Benjamin Brodie, William Sharp

A Letter to Sir Benjamin C. Brodie, Bart., P. R. S.

in reply to his letter in

Benjamin Brodie, William Sharp

A Letter to Sir Benjamin C. Brodie, Bart., P. R. S.
in reply to his letter in

ISBN/EAN: 9783337780692

Printed in Europe, USA, Canada, Australia, Japan

Cover: Foto ©Andreas Hilbeck / pixelio.de

More available books at **www.hansebooks.com**

A LETTER

TO

SIR BENJAMIN C. BRODIE, Bart., P.R.S.,

IN REPLY

TO HIS LETTER

IN

'FRASER'S MAGAZINE' FOR SEPTEMBER, 1861.

BY

WILLIAM SHARP, M.D., F.R.S.

"Truths which the theorist could never reach,
But observation taught me, I would teach."
COWPER.

SECOND EDITION.

LONDON:
HENRY TURNER AND CO., 77, FLEET STREET, E.C.
MANCHESTER:—41, PICCADILLY, AND 15, MARKET STREET.

MDCCCLXI.

PREFACE.

THE Medical Profession throughout the world is at present divided by a great controversy.

Much prejudice and animosity are exhibited on both sides, which cannot fail to damage the whole body. No one can regret this more than I do.

While desiring to live peaceably with all, I am reluctantly involved in this professional warfare. I would gladly accomplish a reunion.

In the hope of removing some misapprehensions from the minds of the leading members of my profession, I wrote to Sir B. Brodie two years ago, requesting an interview, and asking him to invite any other medical men he might judge expedient to be present.

I addressed him as President of the Medical Council, and as President of the Royal Society, and his reply was to the effect that his professional engagements were very few; but he was busy about other matters, and had no leisure to answer my letter then, but he would do so at some future time.

Sir Benjamin's letter in the 'Fraser' of last month, is his next communication; one object of which seems to be to fix upon me personally the contemptuous appellations of "empiric" and "pretender," which he had before applied to homœopathists in general.

The only other names Sir Benjamin mentions are those of Hahnemann and Curie. With the principal writings of the former I have made myself thoroughly familiar; those of the latter I have not seen, not being aware that they were of any special interest.

Several replies to Sir B. Brodie's letter have been sent to me, for which I beg to return my thanks. I have refrained from reading them while engaged upon my own, but shall read them with pleasure now that this is completed.

Very possibly the same facts and arguments have been brought forward by others, and in a better manner. I should have been well contented to leave the matter in their hands, if I had not been assured that an answer would be expected from me, I being the only person living to whom Sir Benjamin refers by name.

I should have been glad of more time and leisure for the writing of my answer ; it might, perhaps, then have been more worthy of the attention of my profession and of the public, but it must appear as it is, and be taken for what it may be worth.

Since the remark made on page 47 was printed, my publisher has informed me that some of the medical journals have admitted an advertisement of this Reply. I hope this is some evidence of the approach of a better state of feeling.

I hear that disappointment has been expressed at the tardy appearance of my Reply, which I much regret ; but it has not been possible to get it written, printed, and bound, more quickly.

That I may be guilty of no unfairness, I have reprinted Sir B. Brodie's letter, with other letters, in an Appendix.

HORTON HOUSE, RUGBY;
October 30th, 1861.

The first Edition having been exhausted in a week, a second is at once called for, and is issued with very little alteration.

CONTENTS.

A LETTER

SIR BENJAMIN C. BRODIE, Bart., P.R.S.

I.

MY DEAR SIR BENJAMIN,

1. IN former years I have experienced occasional acts of kindness from you, which I do not forget; and I desire to retain the feelings of regard for you which they produced in me at the time. You have now published a letter in which, referring to me by name, you intimate to the world that I am become an empiric and a pretender. I am called upon to reply to this letter, but I hope to do so in a spirit animated by the recollection of former kindness, rather than in that which such an injury might be expected to excite.

I have applied for permission to send a temperate reply to be inserted in 'Fraser'; but this act of justice and fairness has been refused me by the editor; there remains, therefore, only the alternative of an independent publication.

Others will characterise as it deserves, this refusal

on the part of the journal which has inserted your criticism of a system of medicine, and of those who have adopted it ; the obstacle thus raised affords me the opportunity of being less brief, and gives me leave to attend also to a wish of yours, implied by what you said on the occasion of your election to be President of the Royal Society, in 1858. We had then some conversation in the Society's room, and on my ' Investigation of Homœopathy' being mentioned, you made this remark to me, " you have not told us enough." I shall now both answer your letter, and also tell you somewhat more on the same subject.

We will, if you please, sit down together, and endeavour to go through our discussion in good humour. Had you invited me to an interview, before publishing your letter, this might have been undertaken in private ; and such an invitation, on your part, would have been a proof of friendly consideration towards a professional brother, who, in your judgment, had fallen into error ; and, on my part, would have been appreciated and acknowledged as such. But, since you have acted otherwise, and have publicly condemned me, I am under the necessity of defending myself with equal publicity.

2. You commence thus, addressing a friend ; " You desire me to give you my opinion of what is called Homœopathy.   *   *   *   I have made myself sufficiently acquainted with several works, especially those of Hahnemann, the founder of the homœo-

pathic sect, and those of Curie and Sharp. The result is, that, with all the pains I have been able to take, *I have been unable to form any very distinct notion* of the system which they profess to teach."

This being so, I cannot help expressing surprise that you did not here close your letter. Under the conviction that it was a subject you did not yet understand, how could you feel justified in writing more? Did it not strike you that the confidence of your readers must be shaken by this acknowledgment? As, in another place, you repeat the confession that you "cannot comprehend" it, and, in still another, that it is "wholly unintelligible," your meaning cannot be misapprehended ; and, in the minds of many, this consideration alone has disposed of your letter altogether.

3. To those who have not found the subject unintelligible, the inference can scarcely be avoided, that the amount of reading you have held to be "sufficient," has been but a slight and imperfect perusal. If this be so, it is another reason why it would have been prudent to have kept silence. As regards my 'Investigation of Homœopathy,' the book we have now to deal with, I am well persuaded, that, had you given it a serious and impartial reading, you could not have designated the facts as "scanty," nor the reasoning as "puerile and illogical;" nor could you have classed me, for writing it, among "empirics" and "pretenders." It will not be difficult, I think, to

bring others to the same conviction ; and thus, if it appear that *you have read little of the book you condemn*, your letter will be laid aside for a second reason.

4. Moreover, a third and an unanswerable ground of objection to your letter appears in the obvious consideration that no amount of mere reading is " sufficient" to qualify you to give an opinion upon the matter.   It is an *experimental* question, and no one, who has not repeated the experiments, however well informed he may be upon other topics, is competent to offer an opinion, much less to pronounce an adverse judgment upon it.   Would a chemist be permitted to question or deny the results obtained in the laboratory of another chemist, unless he had himself repeated the experiments, and could not obtain the same results ?   Certainly not, you will say : neither is a medical man justified in denying the experience of another, who has not himself tried the same remedies in similar cases.   Did you acquire your surgical experience, and deserved reputation, by the reading of books ?   And would you criticise another surgeon, whose experience differed from your own, if that experience was founded upon a mode of operating which you had not yourself tried ?   Assuredly not, you will reply.   And should not a similar course of procedure be pursued in the matter of *medical*, as in that of *surgical* treatment ?

For the reason, then, that *you have not made experiments* or practical observations in your own hands, and under your own eyes, nor even witnessed them in the hands of others—either of which, if done, you were bound to record—your whole letter, and whatever further you may have said on the subject, may be dismissed, without injustice as of no weight.

Suffer me to repeat, that this is not a matter which admits of *à priori* reasoning. It is one of experiment and observation ; and until you personally try these experiments, and make these observations, however much we may respect your judgment upon affairs you are conversant with, your opinion upon this subject is of no value. Forgive me, Sir Benjamin, for speaking thus plainly ; I mean it not uncourteously. I feel as John Hunter did when he wrote to Jenner,—" *Why think ? Why not try the experiment ?*"

5. It is due to you to remark that the deficiency of information I complain of, is shared by every medical writer against homœopathy I have yet met with. All are unacquainted with the subject, *as a practical inquiry*. The truth is, that all those who have given it a fair and sufficient practical trial have been, on the whole, so well satisfied with its results, that they have adopted it as their future mode of practice. The conversion of all investigators of the new method has been so remarkable, that, a few years ago, it was thought necessary to meet it with such advice and admonition as the following :—" We warn the man that is inclined to investigate this folly against experimentation on the subject, which *will be*

almost sure to end in his adopting the delusion.'' What singular distrust! Such a folly and delusion as this is represented to be, ought to dread the exposure of an experimental investigation. But these warnings having proved insufficient to stay the progress of the reformation in medicine, the colleges and medical societies now make it a matter of compulsion to their members not to meddle with it, or rather of expulsion to those who dare to do so. For proof of this I refer to the resolutions of colleges given in the latter part of this reply, and to letters in the Appendix.

Nevertheless, a large number of intelligent practitioners have had the moral courage to act conscientiously and independently, notwithstanding such warnings and threats; they have given the system a practical trial; they have thus been induced to lay aside their former mode of practice, and have adopted the new one; and they have published the cases which have led them to make the change. The facts thus published outweigh all the assertions opposed to them.

6. No sufficient trials have been made and published on the other side. *You* will not, I am sure, mention those of Professor Andral, but as they are still brought forward by others, with an air of triumph, I hope you will pardon me if I notice them in this place. Their entire want of value has been repeatedly shown, particularly by Dr. Irvine,* seven years ago.

* ' British Journal of Homœopathy ' for 1844.

They are, notwithstanding, still appealed to, their character misrepresented, and their importance exaggerated, so that this want of value must be shown again.

They were made in the Hôpital de la Pitié, in Paris, in 1834, under unfair and unfavorable circumstances; moreover, no practitioner of homœopathy appears to have been present; and the report was drawn up by one of Andral's pupils, who, as well as M. Andral himself, was strongly prejudiced against the method.

At the risk of being tedious, but to stay charges of unfairness, I shall present the report of the cases entire; it will then, I think, need little comment on my part to show how worthless the trial was, and how unworthy of the name of Andral.

It appears that *one dose* only, and that an infinitesimal one, of the medicine named, was given in each case, and how much was considered a dose is not stated. If the patient was not cured in a few days, the result was reckoned a failure.

Little care seems to have been taken even with the diagnosis, as may be seen without looking beyond the first case; and no care at all in prescribing for the actual disease. A single symptom, often having little if any, connection with the principal malady, was arbitrarily isolated from the rest—I wonder why!—and a medicine was almost as arbitrarily chosen for it. A cure was to follow, or the method was to be condemned.

It will be noticed, also, that a large proportion of the

cases were incurable or unmanageable chronic diseases; such as hemiplegia, gout, dropsy of the pericardium, other diseases of the heart, and even three cases of phthisis. It cannot but be admitted that such diseases are not adapted to be test cases of any method of treatment. It could not be for lack of more suitable cases that these were selected, for the trial was carried on for thirty-five weeks, and was made in a large hospital.

The cases were thirty-five in number.

M. ANDRAL'S CASES.[*]

"ACONITE, 24th dilution.

"1. Patient aged 25.   Disease, gastritis; predominating symptom, intense fever.   Effect, the pulse fell two beats in twenty-four hours; next day, the eruption of small-pox appeared.

"2. Intermittent fever of a quotidian type; predominant symptom, action of the heart.   No effect.

"3. Acute angina; predominant symptom, intense fever.   Effect, diminution of the sore throat, and falling of the pulse.

"4. Phthisis; predominant symptom, frequency of the pulse.   Effect, falling of the pulse.

"5. Acute arthritis; predominant symptom, frequency of the pulse.   Effect, a violent headache.

[*] 'Bulletin Général de Thérapeutique,' Sept., 1834.

"ARNICA, 6th dilution.

" 6. Pulmonary symptoms; predominant symptom, great giddiness. No effect.

" 7. Cerebral congestion; predominant symptom, violent vertigo. Effect, the patient said he experienced immediate relief.

" 8. Hydro-pericarditis; predominant symptom, giddiness. No effect.

" 9. Dysmenorrhœa, with chronic gastritis; predominant symptom, very violent headache. No immediate effect; improvement on the third day.

"BELLADONNA, 24th dilution.

" 10. Hemiplegia; predominant symptom, confusion of sight. No effect.

" 11. Bronchitis; predominant symptom, violent cough. No effect.

" 12. Bronchitis; predominant symptom, violent cough. No effect.

" 13. Affection of the optic nerve; predominant symptom, considerable confusion of sight. No effect.

" 14. Heart disease; predominant symptom, giddiness. No effect.

"BRYONIA, 30th dilution.

" 15. Intermittent fever; predominant symptom, flying pains. No effect.

" 16. Hypertrophy of the heart; predominant symptom, acute pain at the epigastrium. No effect.

" 17. Acute arthritis; predominant symptom, pain at the shoulder. No effect.

" 18. Pleurodynia, with bronchitis; predominant symptom, continued fits of coughing.   No effect.

" 19. Chronic gastro-enteritis; predominant symptom, violent pain in the left knee and shoulder.   No effect.

" COLCHICUM, 15th dilution.

" 20.   Acute arthritis; predominant symptom, violent pain, with redness and swelling of both wrists. Effect, abatement of the pains.

" 21.   Lumbago; predominant symptom, violent pain in the loins.   No effect.

" 22. Tubercular consumption; predominant symptom, stitch in the left side.   Effect, abatement of the pain.

" HYOSCYAMUS, 12th dilution.

" 23. Pulmonary consumption; predominant symptom, violent cough.   No effect.

" 24. Pleurisy with bronchitis; predominant symptom, violent cough.   No effect.

" 25. Bronchitis; predominant symptom, violent cough.   No effect.

" MERCURIUS SOLUBILIS, 6th dilution.

" 26.   Mercurial trembling of upper and lower limbs.   No effect.

" 27. Syphilis, ulcerations.   No effect.

" NUX VOMICA, 24th dilution.

" 28.   A woman aged 21.   Dysmenorrhœa, with

chronic gastritis; predominant symptom, very great dyspnœa. No effect.

"29. A woman aged 22. Dysmenorrhœa, with chronic gastritis; predominant symptom, dyspnœa. No effect.

"30. A woman aged 18. Amenorrhœa; predominant symptom, inclination to vomit. No effect.

"PULSATILLA, 24th dilution.

"31. Chronic gastro-enteritis; predominant symptom, diarrhœa. Effect, sensible improvement.

"32. A woman aged 22. Chronic gastritis; predominant symptom, diarrhœa with colic. No effect.

"CHAMOMILLA, 12th dilution.

"33. Diarrhœa, without colic. No effect.

"OPIUM, 6th dilution.

"34. Affection of the uterus and the heart; predominant symptom, obstinate constipation (!). No effect.

"PLUMBUM, dilution not stated.

"35. Obstinate constipation, which has lasted eight days. No effect."

Such are Professor Andral's famous experiments. Many observations crowd upon the mind while reading them, but I must content myself with noting two or three.

First. Hahnemann never practised, nor taught such a method as this; hence the experiments are nugatory.

Second. The value of the principle upon which drugs are to be prescribed, is quite distinct from the efficacy of the infinitesimal dose, and they ought to be tested separately; as is again and again explained in the 'Investigation.' On this ground, also, the experiments are nugatory.

Third. There is so little skill shown in the selection of the remedies, that the wonder is, not that so many produced no effect, but that, in seven or eight instances, beneficial effects followed. It might be argued that these positive results are really of more weight than the remaining negative ones.

Lastly. To close the whole affair, Andral himself subsequently condemned them, acknowledging that they were unavailing for the object proposed.

7. Hahnemann published his 'Organon,' or new method, in 1810; and, as you own (in the 'Quarterly Review'), instead of his method being submitted to trial, he was subjected to "a most unjustifiable perse-cution." Not until 1834, twenty-four years afterwards, is this unworthy attempt at experiment made by M. Andral; an attempt in which a caricature rather than a trial of homœopathy is exhibited; after nearly thirty years more, a space of half a century altogether, these are the solitary experiments appealed to, for the purpose of crushing a system of medicine, which, during this same space of time, has spread over all the civilised world!

You accuse us of asserting principles " on the

evidence of the most doubtful and scanty facts." The whole republic of medicine have nothing to appeal to against us, but these meagre and worthless experiments of Andral. I marvel that they thus expose the nakedness of their land. You, Sir Benjamin, are wiser, in that you make assertions without adducing the evidence of *any facts at all*. Yes, Sir Benjamin, the assertions are on your side, but the facts are on our side, and against you. You will not, I hope, reply in the words of a certain illustrious personage, " Are they ?—then so much the worse for the facts ! "

8. It might here be submitted to any competent and unprejudiced judge that you have failed to make out a *primâ facie* claim to be heard, so that your case may, with justice, be put out of court ; but, as you are not of this mind, and have written against the system of medicine I have adopted and recommended, I am compelled to write further in its defence. I proceed, therefore, to notice next, your very persevering endeavour to raise a prejudice against this method of treating diseases, by classing it with quackery and fraud, and by denominating its advocates empirics and impostors, " who very probably never studied disease at all."

This plan you have pursued, Sir Benjamin, for twenty years. In 1842, you wrote an elaborate article in the ' Quarterly Review.' In 1856, in the ' Medical Times and Gazette,' you referred your readers to this article in the ' Quarterly.' And now, in 1861, you

take the trouble to write an epitome of this same
article for 'Fraser's Magazine.' In this last paper
you add my name to the two previously given, with
whose books, you say, you have made yourself "sufficiently" acquainted. It ought not to be without
some indignation that I ask you to point out a single
passage in the 'Investigation' which savours of
quackery or of fraud.

Before that book was written, by your own acknowledgment, as appears in the book itself, I was a worthy
member of the medical profession; and I demand of
you either to support your accusation by proof, or to
retract it. Let us inquire what the book professes to
be:—"An Investigation of Homœopathy." The examination of this medical system is represented as
taken up with reluctance, and from a sense of duty,
and pursued with industry for several years. The
book contains an independent opinion of the matters
investigated; it assures the reader that "I have
noticed every feature of Hahnemann's exposition of
his system, and there is not one which I admire, or
can adopt in the terms in which they are propounded
by him. As expressed in his writings, they all, without exception, excite in my mind a strong repugnance."
It is added, that "I may be supposed to be a disciple
of Hahnemann, and be held responsible for his follies.
I altogether disclaim such responsibility and relationship."

In this book are the results of several years of very
careful observation; the facts are given as they pre-

sented themselves to me in the course of the inquiry; and the opinions are inferences drawn from these facts. These opinions were left open to be modified by further research; but, at the time, they were honestly entertained, and faithfully recorded; and this record was given in the plainest language I could use, and without reservation or concealment. All this was done in the spirit of the motto of the book, which is a sentence from William Harvey—a name never to be mentioned without reverence—" I claim that liberty which I willingly yield to others, the permission, namely, in subjects of difficulty, to put forward as true such things as appear to be probable, until proved to be manifestly false." And is it just, Sir Benjamin, when your patients come to me, as they occasionally do —is it just to tell them they leave you in favour of a " homœopathic doctor, who, very probably, never studied disease at all ? "

You refer your friend to my book, as well as to those of Hahnemann and Curie, and you rank me along with them as an empiric and a pretender. I also gladly refer to the same book, and am not afraid to abide the judgment of every honest and unprejudiced reader.

You are offended because " Hahnemann treats the subject in one way, Curie in another way, and Sharp in another way still." But is there anything unusual or unreasonable in this ? When a new subject of study is first introduced, is it not always looked at from different points of view by early investigators ?

Are there to be no independent thinkers in medicine?
I respect you much, Sir Benjamin, as formerly President of one of our colleges, but you must pardon
me if I decline to submit to your dictation in matters
of science.   I am loyal as can be wished, and desire
to render to all their due; but tyranny in the region
of knowledge has reigned long enough.   "Amicus
Socrates, amicus Plato, sed magis amica veritas."

You make many sensible observations upon quackery,
but they are beside the mark.   The new method of
medical treatment is not quackery; it has no secrets,
it has purchased no patent.   Like other medical systems, it may be practised in an empirical manner; and
there may be pretenders and quacks, who hope to gain
by using its name; but, alas! what part of the profession is free from such unwelcome intruders?

The new method may have errors in it, and it is
the duty of those who can discover such errors to point
them out; no one has done this more freely than myself; but medical errors are not criminal, except when
they arise from culpable negligence, as you remark in
your letter, "humanum est errare."

You are in error, whether culpably or not, others
will judge, when you put down the whole method as
"absurd and nonsensical," and all its advocates as
quacks and pretenders.   You are plainly in the wrong
when you apply such terms of reproach to men who
have enjoyed the same liberal education, who have
pursued with the same good conscience the path of
professional duty, and who are the objects of as much

confidence and esteem from those who know them, as yourself.

To conclude an unpleasant subject, and one which, though keenly felt by the profession, is not cared for by the public. The new method, even if it could be proved to be erroneous, is far removed from empiricism, and never can be justly condemned as such. And, though there are disreputable persons, who call themselves homœopathists, and seek by this to further their selfish ends, there are also men who have the same claim to be acknowledged to be professional men of respectability and honour as yourself, and whose testimony is as worthy of credit as your own. I cannot, therefore, avoid again remarking that the language you have suffered yourself to use is untrue, because it is misapplied, and that you should regret having made such charges, and retract them.

9. We now arrive at something more agreeable —the success of the new method. " But, however this may be," you had been speaking of its inefficiency, " I may be met," you go on to say, " by the assertion, that there is undoubted evidence, that a great number of persons recover from their complaints, under homœopathic treatment, and I do not pretend in the least degree to deny it."

It is well you are willing to admit this success as an undeniable fact; it is very comfortable that this need not be a subject of discussion between us; I wish we were as well agreed upon all the other features of the question.

But there may be different ways of accounting for this success, and you may account for it in one way, and I in another; it becomes necessary, therefore, to inquire what reasons you give for the success of this treatment in individual cases, and for its spread over the world.

As I have noticed in another place, you offer three reasons.

First, spontaneous recovery; "the living machine has the power of repairing itself. If the arts of medicine and surgery had never been invented, by far the greater number of those who suffer from bodily illness would have recovered, nevertheless." This doctrine differs from that which medical men have usually held; but, admitting it to be true, homœopathic treatment, not interfering so much with nature as other methods do, must really be the best. In all cases which can recover spontaneously, strong dosing and active counter-irritation must rather hinder than help. The homœopathist at least lets his patient get well, while another practitioner, if he does not do worse, at any rate prolongs his patient's illness, by interfering more than is necessary with nature's proceedings. It is well that this should be understood by medical men, as well as by patients, that, on your own showing, and in your own words, "whenever homœopathy is a substitute for bad treatment, *it must be the better of the two."* And seeing that patients will seldom be content without treatment of some kind, this is a large admission. But—

Secondly, "this does not account for all the success of homœopathy;" there is the large class of imaginary or exaggerated ailments. "It is astonishing," as you say, "to what an extent some persons contrive to imagine diseases for themselves; * * * and such feelings will disappear as well under the use of globules as they would under any other mode of treatment, or under no treatment at all." For this class of sufferers you thus admit that homœopathy is at least as good as any other treatment. For the

Third reason, you mention cases in which medical men have made mistakes in their diagnosis and treatment. "If it should so happen that a medical practitioner, from want of knowledge, or from a natural defect of judgment, makes a mistake in his diagnosis, and the patient whom he had unsuccessfully treated afterwards recovers, * * * and the recovery takes place under the care of a homœopathist, or any other *empiric, * * * we really cannot very well wonder, that, with such knowledge as they possess* of these matters, *the empiric should gain much credit with the public."*

Why should you descend to such language as this? Have we not been educated in the same school? You are the older and more eminent member of our common profession, but I do not yield to you in the love of that profession. The empiric, you say, has knowledge,—of what kind? Where did he obtain it?

Is it not similar to your own, and has it not been acquired in the same manner? And, in the case you have supposed, it is used to better advantage for the patient. Is it consistent with reason or justice to call one practitioner, who, *from want of knowledge*, makes a mistake, and unsuccessfully treats the patient, the " regular;" and the other, who, *by more knowledge*, corrects the mistake, and cures the patient, the " empiric ?"

To return to the causes assigned by you for the success of homœopathy. It is to be remembered that in all these large classes of cases, including those which will of themselves naturally recover; those which are more or less imaginary; and those in which the physician has made a mistake; in all these cases, and they must form a large proportion of the actual amount of illness, you admit that homœopathy is as good as, if not better than any other treatment. May not the public be congratulated in having met with educated medical practitioners, who can so often cure them with so much comfort and safety?

There remains only one class of cases unconsidered. In 1842, you say, " If they (homœopathic remedies) have the virtue of being in themselves innocent, no harm can result from their use where nothing is wanted, or nothing can be done; but it is quite otherwise on those occasions which call for active and scientific treatment, and we have good reason to say that many individuals have lost their lives from trusting to their use under these circumstances." In 1861, you repeat this sentiment in these words: "There are numerous cases in which spontaneous recovery is out of the question; in which sometimes the life or death of the patient, and at other times the comfort or discomfort of his existence for a long time to come, depends on the prompt application of active and judicious treatment. In such cases homœopathy is neither more nor less than a mischievous absurdity; and I do not hesitate to say that a very large number of persons have fallen victims to the faith which they reposed in it, and to the consequent delay in having recourse to the use of proper remedies."

Now this is the point of your letter—it is written to alarm and to deter; but it is just what you *ought* to hesitate to say, for you do not know it to be true. I am very anxious to avoid saying anything uncourteous, but I am persuaded that you cannot sustain this assertion by facts. It has been much observed by your non-medical readers, that you do not advance a single example or fact in proof of one of your many assertions. For example, you assert that homœopathy is a mischievous absurdity; but you have not tried one experiment with its remedies, and do not know that, instead of being mischievous, they are efficacious in the cases you have just now referred to, beyond any other. You assert of my book, that the reasoning is puerile and illogical; but you do not quote, or refer to, a single sentence in proof. You say that in all times there have been pretenders, and imply that I am one of them; but you do not advance an item of any kind, in support of an accusation which, without proof, is a calumny. And so here you assert that "a very large number of persons have fallen victims," without any statements or references in proof. As I have already remarked, you condemn me for making statements on the evidence of scanty facts, but you out-do me in this, and make all these assertions without the evidence of any facts.

No, Sir Benjamin, you have been misinformed, very large numbers of persons do *not* fall victims to homœopathic treatment. Here is issue joined between the parties, and the *onus probandi* rests upon you.

The truth, on the contrary, is that in sudden and acute disease, where no time is to be lost, the recoveries are far more numerous, and much more expeditious under the new method, than under anything you wish us to understand by the term " active treatment." In proof of this I refer to cases in the 'Essays,' and to my daily practice for the last twelve years.

Again, as to serious chronic disease, it is equally true that many cases considered to be incurable by the usual modes of treatment have been cured by the homœopathic remedies. I think you must remember one or two yourself; and I may again refer to the ' Essays,' to my own practice, and to that of every respectable practitioner who makes use of similar remedies. I should be sorry to appear to boast, but your letter compels me to say that I have seen cases of asthma, of epilepsy, of hæmorrhage, of tabes mesenterica, of diabetes, of scirrhus, of abscess of the kidney, and of other serious diseases, which were incurable in the hands of their former medical advisers, recover. I am aware that it is objected to statements like this, that they are far surpassed by those of Holloway or Parr, and that they weigh as little in the minds of medical practitioners. Pity that these last should be so blinded by prejudice that they can see no other difference between the experience of physicians, and the advertisements of nostrum vendors.

I would also earnestly call your attention to the value of the new treatment in the diseases of *children* —the bright jewels in the family circle. How mercifully gentle, how conspicuously efficacious, in their severest sufferings it is, only daily experience can adequately teach.

Nor is the effect of the same treatment, transferred to the diseases of the lower animals, to be overlooked. It is a fact which bears a direct and powerful testimony in contradiction to your assertions. Many gentlemen have their horses treated exclusively by this method; many farmers are thankful for it for their cattle and sheep. I am informed that more than one dairy in London, and many in the country, are glad of its benefits. The recoveries of cows attacked with pleuro-pneumonia, an epidemic so prevalent of late years as to be known as the "lung disease," and, under all other treatment so fatal, have been numerous and remarkable.

To return to my own experience, it is no more than bare justice to say, that I have had much better success in the results of treatment, since I became acquainted with these remedies than I had before; and for the character of my previous position, I take the liberty to refer you to the town and neighbourhood where I formerly resided, and from which I retired because I had not health and strength to get through the work.

You admit the superiority of the homœopathic over the usual treatment, in a very large number of complaints; it is, you say, the better of the two. In the remaining cases, from your present inexperience, you are very naturally afraid to trust it; you think it would not be sufficiently efficacious. In reply, I beg to assure you, that twelve years of daily practice with these remedies have convinced me that your fears upon this point are groundless, and that in these remaining cases, as well as in the others, *it is the better of the two.*

So much for this part of our subject, the success of homœopathy, and the reasons which may be assigned for it. That it has been a progressive success is evident from your own writings. In your article in the 'Quarterly,' a certain amount of prevalence of the method is implied; but it is plainly acknowledged in your letter in 'Fraser.' From this we may gather, that you are aware that, notwithstanding you then wrote so strongly against homœopathy, in the hope, doubtless, of checking its progress, the success it had attained in 1842 has been *greatly on the increase* during the twenty years which have since elapsed.

10. But if the success of homœopathy has been progressive, so also has been the prejudice of medical men against it. It may be of service to inquire into the origin of this dislike, and the reason of its continuance; and whether there may be any means of removing it.

The German physician, Hahnemann, the originator of what he called *homœopathia*, first conceived the notion of it in 1790, and published the first paper on it in ' Hufeland's Journal,' in 1796. This journal was well known as the leading medical periodical of Europe, at that time. There seems to have been no feeling one way or the other, on either side, at this commencement. The notion of *similia similibus curantur* was the result of an earnest endeavour, perseveringly followed out, to answer the question which, on engaging in practice as a physician, rose up with great power in his mind,—" How is it possible, with conscientious fidelity, to discharge my trust? Is there no great principle by which I can guide my course ?"

His propositions were novel, and opposed to the bias of thought which the professional mind had yielded to for many ages. A difficulty in apprehending their meaning, and an unwillingness to give attention to them, were naturally the first results of their appearance; and neglect and delay were the consequences of these. In the irritable mind of the proposer, this neglect and delay gave rise to impatience; the conviction that he had discovered a truth of high value to mankind increased his self-esteem, and led him to press his reform with an unwise eagerness; and the two together tempted him to use words of disparagement towards his fellow-practitioners which they did not deserve, and which he was not justified in using.

Hahnemann did not remember how much opposition all new truth and all real reformation must encounter; nor how much time must elapse, and how much forbearance must be exercised, before they are accepted by mankind. Channels of education, grooves of thought, and forms of expression are mighty hinderers of progress and improvement; and when to these are added the barriers of prejudice, the tide of fashion, the cries of party, the claims of self-interest, and the necessities of life, progress and improvement are all but impossible. And yet these impediments lie, more or less, in the path to every kind of knowledge; and are met with, and must be surmounted in every field of inquiry. It is not wonderful then, that, though thought is quick, progress and improvement are slow.

Hahnemann did not remember this, and the beginning of strife is as the letting out of waters; when once evil passions have been roused they rapidly spread. He was criticised, ridiculed, and abused; and, at length, as you have yourself expressed it, "a most unjustifiable persecution followed." He was driven from city to city, and was made to feel himself an outcast from society. It was but too natural that these angry feelings should arise in his mind, and be vented in no measured language.

Such, I think, if impartially viewed, will be acknowledged to have been the origin of the estrangement between Hahnemann and his colleagues and contemporaries. As you have reminded us, *humanum est errare;* he should have been more modest, and more patient; they should have been more willing to listen and to investigate. But the storm had now arisen, which was to rage and spread from kingdom to kingdom, and, after more than half a century, to be to-day fiercer than ever. For, while nearly all neglected or condemned, a few began to admire and to follow; these few have been succeeded by an increasing number, who, along with the instruction, have imbibed the spirit of opposition, and so have exposed themselves to the enmity of the still remaining majority.

When Hahnemann had added to his system the infinitesimal dose, it is not surprising that his statements should have been viewed with increasing suspicion and incredulity by those who had now become his opponents; and some raillery might have been innocently indulged in, which he ought to have borne with good-humour and cheerfulness; but he had not the privilege of being a native of Ireland, and, his choler rising, the justifiable limits of distrust and hesitation, on the opposite side, were quickly overstept, and an implacable hostility against him burst through every bond of reason and charity. Indignant, and,

I fear, even revengeful feelings were soon indulged in
on his side, and pride, dogmatism, and supercilious
scorn became but too painfully visible in his writings.

11. The controversy has now become a social,
rather than a medical question, and the clashing of
interests, and the workings of jealousy, have reduced
both sides to the condition of two political factions;
a state of things I for one very much deplore.

12. Such is the lamentable picture of a house
divided against itself; is there no sponge by which it
can be obliterated?   It is yet possible, it is not yet
too late for the profession to do now what it ought to
have done fifty years ago.   Let it lay aside its prejudices and its self-interested motives, and take up the
question as one of science, and apply its powers of
experimentation and reason,—and no class of men has
greater,—and let it aim at the elucidation and esta-
blishment of truth, whatever that may be.   Hahnemann, at the best, had but a glimpse of the object
before him; it needs to be illuminated and exhibited
much more clearly, and to be drawn out in fuller pro-
portions, and with more correct definitions.

Of course I believe you when you say, " whatever
I may think at present, I had originally no prejudice
either in favour of or against this new system;" and
you will see from what I have now said, that I agree
with you, when you add, " nor do I believe that the
members of the medical profession generally were, in

the first instance, influenced by any feelings of this kind." What I earnestly desire is, that you, and others of our medical fraternity who, with you, are now, as the sentence just quoted admits, so strongly prejudiced against the new method, the origin and progress of which prejudice I have just related, would return to your former state of unprejudice, and be willing to undertake *a real, that is, a practical investigation* of it,—each one for himself,—and let your judgment be a fair inference from the facts as they present themselves in the course of the inquiry.

This, I am sure, is a reasonable demand; and compliance with it is the only way by which the quarrel can be ended, the unity of the profession be restored, and the respect and confidence of the public be regained.

Sir Benjamin, we will now wish each other good night, and resume our discussion to-morrow.

II.

" I TRUST that I have sufficient love of science to
lead me to desire nothing so much as the attainment
of truth ; and that I am not so vain as to believe that
none of my views can be erroneous." These senti-
ments I have often admired, and, seeing that the words
are your own, Sir Benjamin, you will not be offended
with me if I remind you of them now ; nor think it
unbecoming in me to express a similar confidence that
I earnestly desire to discover truth, and a similar dis-
claimer of infallibility for my opinions. Your ' Observations on the Diseases of the Joints' have not
been less valued because they were thus introduced to
the notice of our profession ; and that which we
respectively wish to teach on the knotty subject we are
at present engaged in, will not be received with less
consideration should it be uttered in the same spirit.
Let us endeavour to continue our discussion in this
propitious and happy frame of mind.

1. You speak thus :—" I have made myself sufficiently acquainted with several works,   *   *
especially that of Hahnemann, and those of Curie and
Sharp.   *   *   *   But Hahnemann treats

the subject in one way, Curie in another, and Sharp
in another way still." It would lead us too far were
we to undertake an examination of all these books, we
will, therefore, limit our inquiries to the last.

This ' Investigation of Homœopathy' contains a
series of essays which, except the thirteenth, were suc-
cessively written in the years 1851, 1852, and 1853.
They were published as they were written, four in each
of those years, and they enjoyed a large circulation in
England and America. The seventh edition contains
the thirteenth essay, which was written in 1856; this
gives the latest views on the subject which I have yet
published.

With respect to the author of the 'Investigation,'
and his claim to be heard, I would rather be silent. It
is both unwise and unpleasant to be egotistical, or a
satisfactory account of my professional antecedents,
which commenced in the beginning of the year 1821,
could be given; suffice it to say, that I was educated
in the most orthodox manner, and had advantages
and successes sufficient to satisfy any moderate
ambition.

I venture, therefore, and I think it not unfitting, to
ask you to read with me again this ' Investigation ;'
first, because it is one of the books to which you
specially refer your correspondent; and, secondly, that
I may remind you of certain passages in each of the
essays, as we pass them rapidly in review.

2. We will read the preface first, which contains,

among other matters, a sketch of your proceedings and
of my own, with reference to Hahnemann's new medical system; noting, before we commence, two things:
—the one, that up to the moment when our attention
was first directed to the subject, there was no difference
between us, save those of age and distinction, which I
have already mentioned; we were embarked on board
the same college ship, and engaged on the same professional voyage;—and the other, that, seeing neither
of us lays claim to intuitive knowledge, we were, at
starting, equally uninformed on the subject, and were
equally unable to say whether it was valuable or worthless.

In the sketch I have just referred to, we begin by
agreeing that there is no important practical knowledge
but that which is "derived from the only true sources
of all knowledge—observation and experience;" but
we then diverge into two opposite paths. The one
pursued by you is thus described:—

"The first step in Sir Benjamin's direction is to pass
judgment upon the new method, and to pronounce
its condemnation as an imposture, and this, so far as
I can learn, without waiting to try a single experiment himself, or being willing to listen with patience
to any account of the experiments or experience of
others.   *   *   *

"Sir Benjamin's second step is to adopt the ancient
artifice of attempting to vilify and disgrace individuals or subjects, by associating them with what is
known or supposed to be disreputable and vile. Before

arriving at Homœopathy, in the article of the 'Quarterly,' a long list of quackeries is introduced, with no other apparent motive but that of pouring contempt and ridicule upon the subject intended to be added to the list,—with any other view such an enumeration is irrelevant and out of place.   *   *   *.

"The fact of numerous recoveries under homœopathic treatment not admitting of denial, Sir Benjamin's next step is to insist upon 'spontaneous recovery.' Because people have many attacks of disease from which they do not die, but, under any treatment, recover, the inference is suggested that all cases treated homœopathically get well of themselves ; and that all who think otherwise, are as credulous as Dr. Johnson, who is ridiculed for believing in the Cock Lane ghost. *   *   *.

"The fourth step taken by Sir Benjamin betrays his want of practical information on the subject with painful clearness, and shows how far the first false step has led him away from his starting point—'important practical knowledge must be derived from the only true source of all knowledge—*observation and experience.*' When speaking of the dilutions or preparations of drugs used by homœopathists, he says, 'Here we meet with a very great difficulty as to the method by which this extreme degree of dilution of medicinal agents is to be determined ; nor does the most diligent examination of the homœopathic writings enable us to get over it.' Sir Benjamin is then greatly troubled at the contemplation of the

3

thousands of hogsheads of alcohol which the dilutions must require; in which trouble of mind his successor in these calculations, Professor Simpson, of Edinburgh, has greatly sympathised."

For the four corresponding steps taken by myself, I must refer to the Preface itself.

Who will not be surprised to find that, after your attention had been thus called to the weakness of your condemnation of the new method, written by you in 1842, you should re-issue it in 1861? What wisdom can there be in this? You had given the subject no experimental examination when you first wrote; you have given it none since. Why should you compel us to tread again this wearisome and barren path?

3. But since, after twenty years of thinking, you are not able to do more than reproduce the old objections, I must not be weary of repeating the old replies; we will, therefore, proceed to the re-perusal of the first Essay, which tells you what, according to the view I took of it ten years ago, homœopathy professes to be. We there read that homœopathy is not a *novelty*, inasmuch as it is plainly recommended in the Hippocratic writings; that it is not *quackery*, inasmuch as it is no secret nostrum, but courts professional inquiry; that it is not an *uncertainty*, but a well-defined object, capable of being exhibited in a clear and intelligible light, as explained by Hippocrates, in the treatment of mania, and as illustrated in the practice of the ill-used Dr. Groenevelt, who

was committed to Newgate in 1694, by the President
of the College of Physicians—*his own college*—for
prescribing cantharides internally in cases of strangury; still you call those practitioners who have
adopted homœopathy *empirics*, and still say that you
are "unable to form any very distinct notion of it."
The Essay goes on to remark, that homœopathy is
not an *infinitesimal dose*, and that to think so is
" a popular mistake, diligently, though, perhaps, igno-
rantly fostered by the opponents of homœopathy;" that
the principle, embodied and expressed in the name,
says nothing about the dose ; all that the rule requires,
as announced by the Hippocratic writer, being this,
" give the poison as a remedy in disease in *a smaller
dose* than would be sufficient to produce similar
symptoms in a healthy person; "—how much smaller
is a matter of experience.   I remind you that you
read in the same place, and we have reached only
the ninth page, " It should not be forgotten that
homœopathy, as a principle, was discovered by experiments made with ordinary doses, and a man may
be a true homœopathist though he never prescribe
any other ; the nature and effect of the so-called infinitesimal doses are separate questions."

Do you remember reading, on page 12, " Homœopathy is a *practical fact ?*   It is not a speculative
theory to be reasoned upon in the closet, but a fact to
be observed at the bedside ; it is no metaphysical
subject to be logically shown by *à priori* reasoning to
be absurd ; it is not a piece of presumption to be

put down by authority; it is the statement of a fact,
to be examined, like the statement of any other fact,
upon evidence. You are not called upon to sit down
and imagine its possibility or its impossibility; but
you are urgently pressed to observe whether it be
true or not. Hundreds of credible witnesses tell you
that curable diseases are, for the most part, readily
cured by the new method. This is stated as a fact.
Is it true? This is the question. Try the medicines.
Why should you not? The interests of humanity
require it. If they succeed, it is a great blessing; if
they fail, publish the failures. This is the only fair
and honest way to oppose homœopathy, and in no
other way is it likely to be opposed with success."

On page 16, you read—" Homœopathy *is medical
treatment.* It is not the ' do-nothing system' (the
' no-treatment at all '), which it is represented to be by
opponents who thus only betray their ignorance."
And, on page 22,—" Medicine, in the general, is
poison to the healthy frame of man, and a remedy to
that frame when sick; this is admitted by all, and
this is homœopathy in the general. Why not, then,
have homœopathy in detail? Why not first ascertain
what symptoms each poison produces, when taken in
health? And why not give it as a remedy for similar
symptoms in natural disease? Medical men have
been experimenting in the treatment of disease for
many centuries, why not try *this* experiment? Our
opponents admit, in general, what they ridicule and
oppose, when carried out in particulars."

Now, Sir Benjamin, all this, and much more to the same effect, having been said to you in vain in 1851, I do not know that anything more can be said in 1861. If you will not be like Jenner, and follow John Hunter's advice, and try the experiment, there is an end of the matter between us; you will not be satisfied by anything it is in my power to advance. We are old people to compare each other to children; but it is the child's argument to say, " I won't because I won't," and when coming from a child, the only answer is coercion; when coming from such aged and venerable lips as yours, I know not how it should be answered, it can but call forth a lament.

I hear you express a wish to interpose a remark on what was said a short time ago on the infinitesimal dose. In speaking of this in your letter you charge " *some* of the homœopathic writers" only, as holding this to be of great importance, and of course you admit that others do not. I am quite aware of this: but inasmuch as you bind all together in the bundle of empirics and pretenders, and do not acknowledge any exceptions, the admission is of little value. What I have to say upon the small dose will find a more fitting place hereafter.

4. In the second Essay the question of the expediency, or otherwise, of bringing this medical controversy before the public is examined. My own judgment has always been very decidedly against the propriety of thus appealing to the public. The sub-

ject is one so entirely professional that, in my opinion, the discussion of it ought to have been confined to professional circles. We read this : " all are ready to admit that, in the present condition of medicine, an appeal to the public is in itself an evil. But it must be observed that this evil did not originate with the homœopathists. Hahnemann did not take this step ; he published his first essay in ' Hufeland's Journal,' a periodical strictly professional. The step was taken by the physicians who opposed him, who, instead of meeting Hahnemann on their common ground, with arguments and facts, wherewith to refute his opinions, and to show the fallacy of his method, appealed to the public authorities, and, by the aid of this un-professional force, drove him from city to city, and from village to village. And, moreover, this appeal to the public by the allopathic portion of the profes-sion has been continued to the present hour, and is still continued."

Your own letter, just now published in ' Fraser's Magazine,' bears testimony that this observation is still true. In this letter you affirm " that any one, though he may not be versed in the science of medicine, who possesses good sense, * * will arrive at the same conclusion as yourself." This may be so ; but irasmuch as, with all your professional and scientific knowledge, and " with all the pains you have been able to take, you have been *unable* to form any very distinct notion of the system which (either Hahnemann, or Curie, or Sharp) professes to teach ;"

and inasmuch as you are satisfied that unprofessional investigators will arrive at no better conclusion, I am strongly of opinion that their "good sense" will preserve them from the discredit of condemning what, under this hypothesis, they would not comprehend. Were this indeed as you suppose, it would have been wiser not to trouble the public with the difficulty; but, Sir Benjamin, the fact in this case also is against you. Very large numbers of talented and educated people, and possessing good sense, have read the books you refer them to, and have not arrived at the same conclusions as yourself. They have understood homœopathy at least well enough to attain a "very distinct notion" of its practical and beneficial effects; and thus, as is remarked in the Essay, "though the public discussion of medical matters be an evil, good has come out of it."

It was with much regret that I ascertained, ten years ago, that every medical periodical belonging to the old school was absolutely closed against any writer who did not entirely reject and condemn homœopathy. Even advertisements of publications in its favour were excluded; my publisher informed me that he had applied, money in hand, to every medical journal in London, Edinburgh, and Dublin, and the advertisement of my book was refused by them all. It was with much reluctance that I was driven to publish my 'Investigation,' as I then did; and it is with still greater regret that I find myself compelled, by your letter, to write in the same manner again.

I have, however, this consolation, I know that several medical men did read my former Essays, and were induced by them to undertake a practical trial of the new method, and in this manner became converts; and I venture to hope that the same thing will happen again, and be the result of the present publication. The public cannot help themselves better in this matter, than by endeavouring to persuade their medical advisers to overcome their repugnance, and, as a duty, to work at the unwelcome task.

The remainder of this Essay is occupied by the discussion of the four following arguments against homœopathy: from authority; from antiquity; from the majority; and from improbability. I must ask you to re-peruse them in private.

5. The third Essay continues the controversy, and contains a defence of the new treatment against medical writers. Dr. Routh's book, as the best which had then appeared, was selected to represent the ob-jectors. Professor Simpson, of Edinburgh, who has since written, has been well answered by his colleague, the Professor of Pathology in the same university, Dr. Henderson.

Dr. Routh admits, as you do, the success of homœo-pathy. "This system," he says, "has unfortunately lately made, and continues to make such progress in this country, and the metropolis in particular, and is daily extending its influence, even amongst the most learned, and those whose high position in society gives them no little moral power over the opinions of the multitude, that our profession is, I think, bound to make it the subject of inquiry and investigation." Would that this good advice of Dr. Routh's had been followed! Other counsels have prevailed, and the universities and colleges, and medical men in general, have resolved that the unwelcome light shall be extinguished. They have rejected candidates, made bye-laws, passed resolutions, expelled members, engaged periodicals on their side, and now they have succeeded in persuading you to give them the help of your name, that it may be said of the anathema, "*stat magni nominis umbrá.*"

Hear Dr. Routh rebuke these unwise and unworthy proceedings : "Violent opposition to homœopathy can do no good. Abuse, intolerance, cannot be accepted by the world as a fair and philosophical inquiry. These can only call forth new defenders. * * * All doctrines are founded on truth, or what is supposed to be truth. The way to disprove a doctrine is, therefore, not by assailing it as ridiculous or absurd,—a conviction of error can only follow when the foundations upon which it is based are shown to be untenable." Now, Sir Benjamin, the foundations on which our belief in the truth of homœopathy is based, are expe- ments which we have tried, and observations which we have made, and, consequently, however much we may have been misled by these experiments and observa- tions, I must repeat, for the hundredth time, that it is not consistent with the constitution of man to be convinced of this misleading by any process of reasoning or mere argument whatever. A conviction of error can be produced, in such a case, only by other experiments and other observations, made in greater number, and with superior care and skill. If, in such a manner, the foundations of our doctrine can be shown to be untenable, we shall, I am sure, be willing to own ourselves mistaken.

Dr. Routh's book is then analysed under three heads: —1. The consideration of the principle of homœopathy. 2. The question of small doses. 3. The statistics upon which is founded a preference of homœopathy, as the most successful method yet known of treating diseases. All which I ask you, Sir Benjamin, to read again.

Under the last head it is remarked, " in conclusion, the published statistics of homœopathy are of value to medical practitioners, either as preliminary information, to induce them to study the subject, seeing that by them at least a *primâ facie* case for inquiry is made out ; or as a confirmation of their own private trials, if the information come, as it no doubt often does, after that private examination has been made. Still the main reliance is to be placed upon what happens in our hands, and under our eyes. Whatever charges of unfairness or fraud may be brought against other persons, we know whether we ourselves are sincere or not. The subject is too serious, and the consequences too important to each individual practitioner, to allow him to be careless in his own proceedings. He is almost necessarily cautious, and awake to all the sources of fallacy to which he may be exposed." He makes the trial, and becomes the convert.

There has been no rejoinder from Dr. Routh to this reply to his book. I am more anxious to have truth on my side than victory, but this looks like having both.

6. Essays IV, V, and VI. The principle of homœopathy; its limits with reference to disease; its limits with reference to remedies. I propose to invite your attention to the principle, or rule of the new method, in the *third* part of this letter; nevertheless, I think these three Essays deserve a re-perusal. You will find in the first, after some illustrations drawn from the laws or general principles of other branches of physical science, and some evidence that medicine has hitherto been uncertain and unsatisfactory, from the want of such a guide, a series of cases which are given as a sample of the kind of trial the new method has been put to in my own practice. It is useless for you cavalierly to designate these facts "scanty and doubtful;" they are neither the one, nor the other; they are both numerous and certain, and demand respectful consideration; at the same time they are declared to be only a "small portion of my trial of homœopathy."

In the fifth Essay I have cleared away some doubt and confusion as to the application of the principle to *disease*, and have shown that it is adapted to every case, but that there are *parts* of some cases which need help in other ways, mechanical, chemical, or surgical, which help is, of course, to be rendered in the most effectual way possible, by the practitioner in attendance.

In the sixth Essay the subject is examined in a similar manner, with a view to ascertain and define the limits within which the principle is confined in its application to *remedies*. This is a field of inquiry not previously laboured in; the old writers who speak of the rule, do so very vaguely; Hahnemann supposes it applicable through a wide extent of agencies, namely, to the action of diseases upon each other, to the influence of mental emotions, to that of physical agents, such as heat, light, electricity, and magnetism, and to the action of drugs; others have extended its supposed applicability still more indefinitely. In this Essay I have endeavoured to prove that it ought to be understood as limited to the action of *drugs*. This view was, at first, opposed by homœopathists, but it seems to be generally acquiesced in now, and we not unfrequently meet with the expression " law of drug-healing," or, as I prefer to put it, the law of healing by drugs.

As I trust you will read these three Essays again, I will quote from them only the conditions under which the examination and testing of this medical rule were carried on by myself, as this may assist others, when undertaking a similar labour.

The *manner* of my trial is thus described:

" The only trial upon which a statement such as

the principle or law of the new treatment can be
fairly put, is the trial by experiment. This must be
obvious. To argue about it is foolish, and a waste of
time. To experiment upon it is rational. I propose,
therefore, to give the evidence adduced upon such a
trial in my own hands. It has occupied my attention
some years ; it has been made in candour and good
faith, and with, I think, all the conditions requisite
for drawing a legitimate conclusion.

"It has been made, in many cases, without the
knowledge of the patient, and therefore to the exclusion of any possible influence from the imagination.

"It has been made under a much greater variety
of circumstances, and upon patients in more diversified
ranks, ages, and constitutions, than can meet together
in the wards of an hospital.

"It has been made very much with medicines
whose injurious or poisonous symptoms, or effects in
health, were previously well known to me ; these
poisonous symptoms or *effects in health* having been
before learned, without any reference to the medicinal
or *curative effects* of the same drug in disease.

"It has been made with doses of all kinds ; not
only with the infinitesimal one, but with palpable and
ponderable quantities of the substances so tried.

"And I have had the advantage of comparing the
results of the new method so obtained, with those in
my own hands under the old practice, during a previous successful career of many years."

Now, Sir Benjamin, compare this trial of mine with

the only one on your side, that of M. Andral in 1834, and say if they are not rather matters of contrast than of comparison ; and then remember, that a very large number of physicians have made trials similar to mine, which have ended, as mine has done, in their adoption of the rule in their own practice.

7. The seventh Essay is on the 'Provings' of drugs, or experiments with them in health. In this Essay it is remarked that " if *drugs* are *remedies* for disease, it is obvious that some means must be used to discover their various properties : in other words, to learn the effects they are severally capable of producing upon the human body." And it is inquired : 1, What have been the means hitherto adopted for this purpose, and the result ? 2, What new method has been suggested ? and 3, How far this new method has been carried out ?" The answer to the first inquiry is, the giving of the drugs in disease, that is, to patients ; and the result is described, from the most eminent medical authorities, as a failure. The answer to the second query is, that a suggestion was made by Haller, and acted upon by Hahnemann, to give drugs in health ; and so to learn the phenomena producible by them *in a healthy body*, before experimenting with them on the body *in a state of disease*. The reply to the third inquiry is, some account of the indefatigable labours of Hahnemann, their extent, and their imperfections.

You cannot well object to the making of such experiments as · these, having been extensively engaged

in similar ones yourself. It is true that the object you
proposed, in the performance of these experiments, was
different; it was to assist in discovering means likely
to obviate the fatal effects of such drugs when taken
as poisons, in other words, for the discovery of *anti-
dotes;* the same object which the ancients proposed to
themselves in similar experiments; and, moreover,
your trials were made upon the lower animals. But
if it is consistent with true science to perform such
experiments for the objects you proposed, it cannot be
less consistent with it to engage in them for the purpose of becoming better acquainted with the *therapeutic* use of these drugs. Some of the conclusions
you arrived at are of sufficient interest and value to be
worthy of being remembered by practitioners of the
new method; that is, for instruction in therapeutics,
as well as in toxicology. For example:

" Alcohol, the essential oil of almonds, the juice of
aconite, the empyreumatic oil of tobacco, and the
woorara, act as poisons by simply destroying the functions of the *brain;* universal death taking place,
because respiration is under the influence of the
brain, and ceases when its functions are destroyed.

" The infusion of tobacco when injected into the in-
testine, and the upas antiar when applied to a wound,
have the power of rendering the *heart* insensible to
the stimulus of the blood, thus stopping the circulation; in other words, they occasion syncope.

" Arsenic, the emetic tartar, and the muriate of
barytes, occasion disorder of the functions of the *heart,*

brain, and *alimentary canal ;* but they do not all affect
these organs in the same relative degree.

" Arsenic operates on the *alimentary canal* in a
greater degree than either the emetic tartar, or the
muriate of barytes. The *heart* is affected more by
arsenic than by the emetic tartar, and more by this
last than by the muriate of barytes." *

This is very much the kind of information which
we require, concerning the mode and sphere of action
of all drugs ; but, in these experiments of yours there
is an element of doubt, from these being the effects
produced on the lower animals, and not on man ; and
there requires to be added, the effects of smaller quantities of the same poisons.

That our knowledge of the properties of drugs may
be as perfect as it ought to be, the provings must be
made upon ourselves, with the additional information
which can be gained from cases of poisoning. For
this latter purpose no book is more useful than Professor Christison's ' Treatise on Poisons.'

There is nothing so much wanted in medicine as a
materia medica which shall contain a true picture of
the sphere of action of each drug. This picture must
not be like Hahnemann's, made up of dismembered
and detached fragments, and crowded with insignifi-
cant, and often perhaps imaginary sensations, and
other trivial matters which mingle with, and hide the
meaning of the real and important symptoms ; but a
steadily drawn and well-defined exhibition of all that

* 'Phil. Trans.' for 1811 and 1812.

is characteristic and specific in the effects which each drug, in its various forms and doses, is capable of producing. For some time I have been attempting this, but it is a work of extreme difficulty and labour.

Such, Sir Benjamin, is what is meant by the "Provings" of drugs; the discovery of their physiological, or, as they are often called, their pathogenetic effects in health, as contrasted with their curative effects as remedies in disease; and the notion which is the foundation of the new method of treating disease, and that which really distinguishes it from all former methods, is this, that there is a relation or connection between these two series of effects. Is not this a "very distinct notion?" There may be different modes of expressing this relation or connection, and some of these modes may be much nearer the truth than others, but the important feature is the relation itself.

Every medical man who embraces the new method is expected to labour in both these fields of experiment and observation;—in the proving of drugs in health, as well as in the administration of them in disease. But in the language of the Essay, "voluntarily to make ourselves ill with poisonous doses of drugs, for the sake of learning, in the first place, upon what organs they act, and the changes they produce on them, and afterwards in what diseases such drugs may be given as remedies, is a painful path, of indefinite extent, beset with obstacles, and demanding an unknown amount of labour and self-sacrifice."

4

In an appendix to this Essay a few cases are given as examples of the Provings.

8. The " single medicine " forms the subject of the eighth Essay.

"The almost stationary condition of the science of medicine has arisen, not only from the natural impediments to the discovery of truth, and from the difficulties peculiar to this subject, but still more from the want of simplicity in the method pursued.

"This method has been defective in two principal particulars, by which the progress of knowledge in the treatment of disease has been effectually hindered.   One of these defects has been the trial of a drug only during the existence of disease, by which its effects are complicated and obscured; instead of first experimenting with it on the body in a state of health, when its own symptoms would appear, unmixed with those of disease.   The other great defect has been the giving of the drug in combination with others, by which its effects are still further complicated and obscured, if not altogether antidoted and prevented, instead of administering it alone, so that its specific action might be produced without let or interference. Had physicians adopted these two proceedings, experimenting in health, and giving the medicine singly in disease, the real properties of each drug might have been, ere this, accurately ascertained."

Read the remainder of this Essay, Sir Benjamin, I think your trouble will be repaid; you will find the advantages of the method not indistinctly pointed out; read carefully what is said on the indications of treatment; and how they are, by giving one remedy at a time, reduced to one indication. Read also the account of another feature by which the new treatment is distinguished from the old, on pages 188-194. How on the old plan *the healthy* parts of the body are disturbed in their natural action, excited, disordered, inflamed, and stupified, and often nothing at all prescribed calculated to act, or intended to act directly upon *the affected part*, whereas, upon the new plan all healthy parts are left undisturbed, and a single remedy is given having a specific action upon the ailing part. Surely, Sir Benjamin, you can form a very distinct notion of the difference between these two methods of treatment. In the one case, artificially produced symptoms are to be added to those of the natural disease; the sick man is to be cured by being made more sick ; in the other case, the natural complaint is to be removed, as a direct effect of the drug which is administered.

Some examples, in illustration of the new practice, are given at the close of the Essay, which ends with the advice of Basil : " The physician should attack the disease and not the patient."

9. Essay IX. "The small dose." Will it be one of the labours of Hercules to get you to take a small dose, Sir Benjamin ? Perhaps so. Some time ago I met one of my allopathic colleagues, an elderly gentleman, and, after shaking hands, I asked him how

he was? "Oh, I am very bad; I have got the diarrhœa." I expressed my sorrow, and inquired, "What medicine have you taken?" "Oh, I never take medicine!" was his quick reply. Is it not so with you, Sir Benjamin? You will not take a small dose, am I right in fancying that you seldom take a large one? Then, read again this ninth Essay with the care and thought which the subject deserves; read it through at a sitting, and, when you have reached the end, tell me, if you then feel disposed to do so, that its reasonings are "puerile and illogical." I will not diminish your pleasure in reading it by making extracts, but I may remind you that its object is to answer the three following questions:

"I. Are we acquainted with any facts which render it probable that infinitesimal quantities of ponderable matter *may* act upon the living animal body? In other words, what does *analogy* teach us?

"II. Are there any facts which show the action of infinitesimal quantities of ponderable matter on the *healthy* body?

"III. What are the actual proofs in support of the assertion that such minute quantities of ponderable matter act remedially on the *diseased* body?"

There are some cases, of both acute and chronic diseases, added as an appendix. The diabetic patient treated in 1850, and who recovered in about six months, is still living and well.

Since this Essay was written a very remarkable discovery has been made in Germany by Professors

Kirchhoff and Bunsen, which has greatly interested all scientific men.   It is, as you are aware, the application of *light*, decomposed by a prism, to chemical analysis.

The discovery is based upon the two following facts :—

Certain substances impart characteristic colours to the flames in which they are heated.   For example,—if a salt of strontium is dissolved in weak alcohol, and the solution is set on fire, the flame is *red;* if a salt of barium, it is *yellow*. This fact is familiarly known.

And when coloured light, thus produced, is analysed by a prism, spectra exhibiting different coloured bands, or *lines of coloured light,* are seen.

These coloured lines are found to be *characteristic* of the substances thus exposed to the high temperature of flame.   They therefore constitute an entirely *new method of chemical analysis*.

The apparatus employed, and the experiments performed with it, are described in the 'Philosophical Magazine' for August, 1860.

To what extent of subdivision the particles of the substances examined by Professors Kirchhoff and Bunsen have been carried, may be learned from a single quotation from the paper I have referred to :

" In a far corner of our experiment-room, the capacity of which was about sixty cubic metres, we burnt a mixture of about three milligrammes of chloride of sodium with milk-sugar (a globule), whilst the non-luminous colourless flame of the lamp was observed

through the slit of the telescope. Within a few
minutes, the flame, which gradually became pale
yellow, gave a distinct sodium line (bright yellow),
which, after lasting for ten minutes, entirely dis-
appeared. From the weight of sodium burnt, and
the capacity of the room, it is easy to calculate that,
in one part by weight of air, there is suspended less
than $\frac{1}{20,000,000}$ of a part of soda-smoke. As the reaction
can be observed with all possible comfort in one
second, and as in this time the quantity of air which is
heated to ignition by the flame is found, from the rate
of issue and from the composition of the gases of the
flame, to be only about fifty cubic cent., or 0·0647
grm. of air, containing less than $\frac{1}{20,000,000}$ of sodium salt,
it follows that the eye is able to detect, with the
greatest ease, quantities of sodium salt less than
$\frac{1}{3,000,000}$ of a milligramme in weight." Similar experiments and calculations were made with lithium, potas-
sium, calcium, and other substances.

Some of these experiments I had the pleasure of
witnessing at one of your *soirées* at the Royal Society's
Rooms, in the spring of this year, and more beautiful
experiments I never saw.

I have made experiments with this apparatus on
the remedies used by homœopathists, which are satisfactory; but this is not the place for their publication.

It is now demonstrated, not only that infinitesimal
particles of known substances exist, but that such
particles can be analysed, and be made to exhibit
characteristic properties. This has been effected in a

manner independent of the careful observation of the action of such particles upon living beings, the only method of examining them previously known. You have doubted and denied the effects produced by minute quantities of matter upon living bodies; you will scarcely question these new experiments with prismatic light. In them the *optic nerve* is impressed by an infinitesimal quantity; and, if one nerve of the living body may be impressed, why not also *other nerves?*

Such is the case (in the legal sense) of the small dose, which, as you observe, "*some* of the homœopathic writers hold to be of great importance."

You will have observed from a perusal of the 'Essays,' that I have always distinctly separated homœopathy from the infinitesimal dose, but I have also thought it right to say what may fairly be said in justification of the use, in practice, of such minute doses of medicine. This, I think, is due to those who have adopted them. But I am not myself an advocate for the frequent employment of what are called the higher dilutions. I prefer giving comparatively substantial doses of the drug which I think is the specific in each case; and this for the following reasons :—

1. Because I wish to have the certainty that I am giving the substance I am thinking about, and intending to give. The higher dilutions, no doubt, may have the drug in them, but, in the preparation of each successive dilution, there must be an increasing possibility of such small particles of the drug being lost.

2. Because the larger doses seem to me generally to do as much good as, and sometimes more than the smaller ones ; and with as little harm. I mean in the hands of a medical man ; they are not so safe in those of an amateur. It is to be understood that the larger doses here spoken of are small compared with the old doses of the same drugs.

3. And because, without forfeiting any advantage, the prejudice against the new method is thereby diminished, and the confidence of the patient is increased.

Let me add one word on the preparation of the dilutions, which you speak of, both in the ' Quarterly' and in ' Fraser,' as if it were an incredible or impossible process. If you will take the trouble to pay a visit to a homœopathic chemist, you may see them made in two minutes. The process is described at page 42 of the ' Investigation.' Some years ago, Dr. Lardner wrote an article to prove that steam navigation across the Atlantic was impracticable ; this was *before* it had been done. What would be thought of him, if he re-published that article now ?

10. Essays X and XI. The " Difficulties" and the " Advantages " of Homœopathy. The former are considered as temporary or permanent ; the latter, as they belong to the physician, or to the patient. I must not make lengthy extracts from these, but I hope you will read them again with attention ; I am sure the subjects deserve this at your hands. " The work of the physician is encompassed with difficulties, his path

beset with obstacles, the struggle he is engaged in, whatever advantages he may at times gain, will always end in his defeat. How happy to meet with any knowledge by which some difficulties may be diminished, some obstacles removed, some new advantages enjoyed! Enough will still remain to try to the uttermost his patience and temper, his industry and perseverance. Were these difficulties, which at times almost lay prostrate the honest labourer in the art of healing, better known and felt, they would enlist on his behalf the sympathies of his fellow-men." Page 251.

The eleventh Essay closes with these words : " Sir Benjamin Brodie formerly entertained respect for me, for he proposed and obtained my election as a Fellow of the Royal Medical and Chirurgical Society, at the time he was President of that excellent society. I have done nothing since to forfeit that respect, except, in the most honest, the most searching, the most distrustful manner, going through this investigation of a new method of treatment, at the request of a medical friend, and at the bidding of my conscience ; it has been no pecuniary or other speculation with me ; it has been the performance of a duty. He calls homœopathy an imposture ; I respectfully ask him to retract that expression, lest he should hereafter suffer in his well-earned reputation, for having unjustly condemned what he did not understand." Page 282.

This friendly remonstrance has been before you, Sir Benjamin, for several years, and you still write with bitterness, and endeavour to brand me as an alien, because "I have sufficient love of science to lead me to desire nothing so much as the attainment of truth," and because this earnest search after truth in medicine has led me to turn aside somewhat from the path of custom and routine. You have written me down an impostor. I willingly acknowledge you to be a distinguished member of the medical profession; but *what has become of your case?* Is it not lost when you take refuge in abuse? Is it not universally admitted that recourse to personalities by an advocate is the strongest proof of the weakness and badness of his cause?

11. Essay XII. "The Common Sense of Homœopathy." I will not take away from the interest of a reperusal of this Essay by making any extracts from it. You shall read it in private. The objects I had before me in writing these twelve Essays were to remove hypotheses while explaining all that admits of explanation, to show that the new method has nothing to conceal, that it is not an obnoxious quackery, but a beautiful science, to publish cases as medical men have always been in the habit of publishing them since the days of Hippocrates, and thus to persuade other physicians to practise this method, not to secure a monopoly of it to myself. Is not this truth, and honesty, and common sense?

12. Essay XIII. Four or five years after the former Essays had appeared, it seemed proper to place

before my friends and readers some account of the further progress my mind had made in this professional inquiry. The results of thought and experience during this space of time are given in the thirteenth Essay, written in 1856. They are described under the following heads :—

" I. I will, first, give some account of those things in the system and teaching of Hahnemann which I reject.

" II. I will recapitulate what my practical trial of homœopathy has led me to acknowledge and accept as true.

" III. I will then state what those parts of the usual method of treating diseases are, the discontinuance of which is involved in the adoption of Homœopathy.

" IV. Lastly, I will point out what those parts of the usual method are, which still remain available and useful, and are to be retained."

I ask your attention, Sir Benjamin, and that of your colleagues, to the contents of this Essay. You will find that the " phantoms of darkness," which hover over and obscure the pages of Hahnemann, are dispersed ; and that statements are made which claim investigation, and are suggestive of new paths of scientific and useful discovery.

I reject the explanation of the principle of homœopathy, as announced in the ' Organon,' as an imaginary hypothesis. I observe that " not only the explanation, but the very definition itself of the homœopathic law

which he gives, has, so far as I can discover, no trust-
worthy evidence to support it. On the contrary, his
statement is open to an insuperable objection, so that
if it really expresses the principle of homœopathy,
that principle itself must be rejected."

And, "as the explanation of the principle of
homœopathy given by Hahnemann is an imaginary
hypothesis, and his definition of it a mere assertion
without proof, so his view of the extent to which it
applies is vague and erroneous. He was apparently
so enamoured with his discovery, and his imagination
was so unrestrained by reason and judgment, that he
could not brook the idea of any limitation of his law;
he would have it to be of universal application." As
I have already remarked, he applies it to diseases
acting upon each other; to the physical agencies
heat, light, electricity, and magnetism; to moral, and
even, as is shown in this Essay, to political influences.
I have given reasons for rejecting all these applica-
tions, and for limiting the investigation of it to its
influence in the physiological and therapeutic action
of drugs.

Many other doctrines of Hahnemann are rejected.

Under the second head I earnestly entreat my
medical brethren to give the following points a
searching and fair trial in their own hands :—

The principle; the provings; the single medicine;
the small dose; the pharmacy.

The principle, as viewed by me at that time, was
expressed in three propositions :

"That each drug selects certain portions or organs of the body upon which to produce its injurious action.

"That the injurious action produced upon the parts or organs of the body thus selected, is more or less peculiar to each drug; that it is characteristic; so that by this action each drug may be known from the rest.

"That drugs are to be given as the best remedies for the diseases which affect the same parts or organs of the body which such drugs affect; and specially when the symptoms manifested by the affected parts or organs resemble the symptoms produced by the drugs."

Such was the issue, at that stage of it, "of my painful examinations of the doctrines of Hahnemann." Why the undertaking of it should have alienated the affections of some of those I most loved, I am unable to understand; but, if I have suffered much in personal feelings, I have kept a good conscience and a quiet mind.

Lord Rosse has observed that, "to the human mind nothing is so fascinating as progress," and it may be added that, in a study so intricate and perplexed as is the philosophy of medicine, nothing is so encouraging. To-morrow then, Sir Benjamin, I shall hope, notwithstanding your prejudice and dislike, to engage your attention, and even perhaps to win your sympathy, by a brief exposition of the progress I am making in this matter.

III.

1. I⊤ is related of John Hunter, whom you and I have the honour to claim as our professional parent, that, when asked with surprise by Sir Astley Cooper, then one of his pupils, whether he had not, the year before, stated an opinion on some point directly at variance with one he had just put forth, he replied, " Very likely I did; I hope I grow wiser every year."

Under the protection of this illustrious example, and in obedience to your implied request to tell you something more, I proceed to explain to you the further progress of thought and inquiry I have been able to make, during the five years which have elapsed since my last Essay was written.

You complain that in the 'Essays' I have not told you enough, and that you are unable to form a distinct notion of the system I have undertaken to teach in them. I purpose, therefore, now to do my best endeavour to make my views of medicine as plain and intelligible as I am at present capable of doing. But, that I may not wander into too wide a field, the consideration of the subject will be limited to an inquiry into the difference between your method and mine.

It will be an advantage, in helping you to understand wherein our views differ, if I take the liberty first to explain your own. If I fail, or be in error in this, I will willingly apologise, and submit to your correction; but, seeing that you have adopted and taught the prevailing method of our time, and that this same method was my own study for thirty years, I shall not be in much danger of mistaking or of misrepresenting it.

2. When our advice is asked by any person suffering from disease, we have three things to ascertain and decide :—the nature of the complaint ; the remedy; and the dose.

3. The *nature of the complaint;* out of many diseases to fix upon the one from which the patient is suffering ;—pathology, nosology, diagnosis. This, according to your view, is best learned by a twofold inquiry, first, into the symptoms, or signs of the internal morbid condition ; and, secondly, into that morbid condition itself. The symptoms are to be gathered by a careful observation of the patient, and by acquainting ourselves with all the information which he and others can give us respecting his ailment. The pathology, or internal morbid condition, is a more difficulty inquiry, and one in which much evil has arisen from mistaken speculations ; it is to be

learned, as well as it may be, by physiological and pathological investigation; that is, by observing, on every opportunity which presents itself, all that can be ascertained of the structure and functions of the internal organs, in a state of health, and during the progress of disease.   In the skin, and external organs, as in the eye, for example, these changes can, to a certain extent, be *seen ;* in the inner parts they are more concealed, but they must as truly exist, and be a legitimate object of scientific research; and, moreover, it must be useful to the physician to know them.

Previous to and up to Hahnemann's time, the want of better knowledge of internal pathology was much to be deplored; little more than vain or hurtful hypotheses prevailed; for example, pain was defined to be " a solution of continuity ;" a rebounding pulse was said to be produced " by the sooty vapours contained in the arteries," and fever " by the pricking of the spiculæ of saline particles."

4. In such a state of things, it is not surprising, though it is much to be regretted, that Hahnemann rejected pathology, and even, as much as he could, the classifying and naming of diseases—nosology—also, and that he should insist that diagnosis should be nothing more than an inventory of the symptoms,—a collection of everything " which can be perceived externally by means of the senses," and nothing more; " only the deviations from the former healthy state

which are felt by the patient himself, remarked by
those around him, and observed by the physician."
According to Hahnemann each case stands alone,
isolated from all others ; the totality of the symptoms
constitutes the disease, and the removal of the symptoms is the cure of the patient.

There are homœopathists, in the present day, who
follow Hahnemann in this. For example, a writer in the
' Monthly Homœopathic Review ' for August, 1859,
teaches thus :—" The homœopathic relation between
the drug and the disease is not this—between the
pathological changes produced by the disease and those
producible by the drug; it is this—the relation
between the symptoms of the disease and those of the
drug. It is a matter of pathognomy, not of pathology."

There may be a sense in which such language is
true, but it is very liable to misconstruction, and so
to lead to the neglect of that serious study of disease
which the physician should, at all times, feel it to be
his duty to pursue ; for this reason I cannot adopt
this language. Thus, then, on the subject of *diagnosis*,
the discovery of the nature of the patient's complaint,
I agree with you, and not with Hahnemann, and
prefer using the old modes of investigation, and,
generally, the old language to express the ideas I
entertain. Pathology and nosology have been dis-
figured by many errors ; they are true sciences notwithstanding, and are worthy of the earnest study of
the medical practitioner.

5. The *remedy;* out of many remedies to select the best—therapeutics, treatment, prescription—that department of medicine in which the need of a complete change has been so long and so deeply felt, as is evident from the strong expressions made use of by the most eminent medical writers for some centuries ; with these you are so familiar that I need not quote them.

I trust we shall carry on the discussion of this part of our subject with lively feelings of interest and pleasure ; nay, I even venture to hope that, before we separate at the close of it, you will have found, perhaps to your surprise, that your unkind feelings towards me have melted away, and that you will be disposed to say, " After all, I have been mistaken about him ; I will once more give him the right hand of fellowship, and I hope he will forgive my past want of charity !"

6. Let me try to exhibit the old and usual method first.

This is based upon two foundations, that of *indications* and that of *intentions.* That is to say, the symptoms of every case are noted, from which the internal morbid condition is inferred ; from this view of the case conclusions are drawn supposed to be nature's indications, and it is believed that a cure will be most speedily obtained, or, if not a cure, that relief will be best afforded by attending to these indications. Medicines are then prescribed with certain intentions, believed to be the best way of attending to these pre-

sumed indications of nature. For example, in the beginning of a fever the shivering, the aching of the back
and limbs, the nausea, the headache, the loss of appetite, and the prostration of strength, are supposed to
indicate the presence of some morbid condition of the
blood and of the secretions ; the indications gathered
from the consideration of this condition or state of
disease are met by prescribing ipecacuanha with the
intention to produce vomiting, blue pill and senna with
the intention to purge, antimony with the intention to
bring on perspiration, saline draughts with spiritus
ætheris nitrici with the intention to increase the secretion of the kidneys ; and thus it is expected, by open-
ing all the "emunctories," to meet the indications of
the case. What follows ? On a subsequent visit the
practitioner finds that the patient has been made very
sick by the emetic, that the bowels have been freely
evacuated by the purgatives, and that the other intentions have been satisfactorily accomplished ; he con-
gratulates himself upon all this, and feels happy in
the reflection that both he and the nurse have done
their duty. Perhaps the patient is not better, perhaps
he is worse ; for this he is sorry, but, attributing it to
the malignancy of the fever rather than to any mistake in the treatment, he becomes only the more
anxious to prescribe again as before, but with increased
vigour. It does not occur to him that his method
may be faulty, or that better success might possibly
follow on the adoption of some other mode of proceeding. So—to give another instance—in the cases of

colic with constipation, the indication is presumed to
be that there is an obstruction which nature calls upon
us to remove, and, with the intention of effecting this,
drastic purgatives are given in quick succession until
the stomach is oppressed by them, the spasm in the
bowels is converted into inflammation, and the vital
powers are exhausted; if, at length, a diarrhœa comes
on, this is taken as a justification of the treatment,
though it be but the prelude to the death of the patient,
which necessarily follows in a few hours. Read also,
as a further example, the indications in Millar's
Asthma, at page 187 of the 'Investigation.'

But let me take a case of your own, for the separation of medical and surgical practice is so arbitrary
and artificial, that this will easily be found. I open
your 'Lectures on the Diseases of the Urinary Organs'
at page 101, and find a case of inflammation of the
bladder. After describing the symptoms you proceed
to the treatment :—

"The disease is to be combated by taking blood
from the arm, or from the loins by cupping, or from
the lower part of the abdomen by leeches." The indication supposed to attach to this case is that inflammatory action must be lessened, and the bleeding,
I presume, is prescribed with the intention of diminishing the flow of blood to the inflamed part. "The
patient's bowels should be kept open by occasional
doses of castor oil." This, I presume, is in obedience
to 'Dr. Hamilton on Purgatives,' and the prescriptive
rights of all Englishmen to be treated according to

the Scotch method; to require purging is understood to be a general indication in all cases. "Opium may be administered with advantage." To give opium when there is pain is as much of prescriptive right as to give aperients in all cases. Pain indicates that something must be done to relieve it; opium is given with that intention, regardless of the mischief it so often occasions, and forgetting that it can generally relieve pain only by stupifying the nervous system, not by lessening the disease which is the cause of the pain. To proceed, in certain cases which you describe, "the patient will derive benefit from the use of mercury—two grains of calomel and half a grain of opium being administered twice or three times daily." The mercury given in this manner is called by the convenient name of an "alterative." The patient being in a very uncomfortable and even dangerous state from severe pain, strangury, &c., the mercury is given to "alter" this.

Thus we have, in your treatment of this case of inflammation of the bladder, the orthodox or "regular," because routine treatment for almost every kind of inflammation, namely, bleeding, purging, opium, and mercury. It is presumed that the indication in inflammation is to lower by antiphlogistics, and the bleeding and drugs just named are prescribed with the intention of effecting this, they being supposed to be the best remedies for this purpose.

But all extremes have their connecting links, and your next paragraph bridges over the gulph between

your method and mine, in a manner worthy of notice.
" In other cases the urine is alkaline, *   *; and
under these circumstances I have known much good
to arise from the use of the *Vinum Colchici*." I suppose you would consider this remedy somewhat in the
light of a *specific;* that is, you would give it because
you know it does good, without knowing why or how,
as sulphur and cinchona are used for their respective
cases. This opens the way for an explanation of my
method.

7. Now, the difference between your practice and
mine is this—that while you are happy to prescribe a
specific in the few cases for which you are furnished
with them, I endeavour to prescribe nothing but
specifics in every case. This is the new method; it
is *the doctrine of specifics;* to seek, and, when found,
to use a specific remedy for every malady. But those
already known to the old practice scarcely reckon up
to half a dozen, and they have been borrowed from
domestic use or from patent medicine vendors, at long
intervals of time between each addition, so that there
is little to be hoped for from a further pursuit of them
in this direction; hence another vast superiority of
the new method, that it not only seeks and uses
specifics, but is furnished with *a means of discovering
them.* " Ah !" I hear you exclaim, " now I have
caught you ! You say, and it is true, that I have
two or three specifics, which I know how to use, but
without knowing why or how they do good; but in

all my other prescriptions I can give the reason why. If I prescribe an aperient or a sudorific, I know why I do so; but now the whole of your practice, on your own showing, is prescribing in the dark; you are ignorant of the action of every remedy you use." Wait, Sir Benjamin, I am not quite so soon silenced, for the next great difference between your system and mine is this, that a reason *can* be given why even specifics do good, and that from the action which is peculiar to and characteristic of each of them.

Such, then, is one view which may be taken of the new method—that it administers specifics in every disease, that is, remedies which are naturally endowed with special properties fitting them to act upon the diseases for which they are given, so as to cure or relieve them. Is this a distinct notion, Sir Benjamin?

Moreover, that it possesses a means of discovering these specifics for diseases for which we were not previously provided with such remedies; and, further—

That it supplies some explanation of the reason why such remedies do good. Are not these distinct notions also?

Again; the old treatment is the method of intentions, to meet certain assumed indications; and the object of this treatment is, by producing increased or additional morbid actions in sundry organs of the body, to cure or relieve the disease; it is thus an *indirect* method of attempting to restore health.

While the new treatment is the method of specifics, the remedy given possessing a natural and efficacious action upon the disease itself; it is thus a *direct* method of cure.

8. We will take another view; the old system generally leaves the diseased organ untouched by the remedies given, and seeks to relieve it on the principle of revulsion or counter-irritation, by producing, artificially, morbid action in parts of the body comparatively healthy, and more or less remote from the principal seat of disease; while the new treatment prescribes remedies having power to act upon the diseased organ itself, avoiding, as much as possible, the production of any disturbance in healthy organs. You leave the ailing parts, and operate upon the healthy ones; we leave the healthy parts undisturbed, and act with our remedies upon the ailing ones. Are not these distinct notions? And which of them commends itself most to common sense? If you say, but I also sometimes give remedies to act upon the part affected, I reply, that when you do so, you practise upon my method, and there is little or no difference between us. Thus, again, upon this view, the old means employed are indirect, while the new ones are direct; the old ones create new ailments, in order to remove or relieve those present, and so increase debility and retard recovery, or at the least prolong convalescence; the new ones let well alone, and act at once upon

the ailing part. I think all these notions are distinct, and I hope you will own that you can understand them.

9. Before proceeding to explain further my own method, having given a fair statement of yours, I think it fitting to remind you of a few of the objections which lie against the old mode. In doing so I shall be very brief. There is—

The difficulty of reading nature's book so as to gather truly what the indications really are; hence the probability that numberless mistakes will be committed in practice by a large proportion of medical men.

There is a similar difficulty, and a similar liability to err, in meeting these indications with suitable intentions.

There is another difficulty in judiciously selecting the remedies best fitted to carry out the intentions when formed.

The obscurity and guesswork of the whole proceeding, and, consequent upon this, the perpetual and hopeless disagreement between medical men, even when engaged in consultation upon the same case.

The mischievous and fatal notion that when the practitioner has accomplished his intentions *he may be content*, even though the patient becomes worse and dies under his treatment. As in surgery it is said, " the operation was most successfully performed, and the patient died two hours after;" so in medicine, when this "active treatment" has been carried out, the friends of the departed are consoled by being told that "everything has been done that could be." I call this notion mischievous and fatal, because it quietens the physician's conscience and encourages an acquiescence in present attainments, while a contrary state of feeling might inspire earnest efforts to discover a better way.

But you reply to this—"The fact is that the fault of the profession for the most part lies in the opposite direction. They are too much inclined to adopt any new theory, or any new mode of treatment, that may have been proposed; the younger and more inexperienced among them especially erring in this respect, and too frequently indulging themselves in the trial of novelties, disregarding old and established remedies." Yes, Sir Benjamin, this is all too true; this error is to be lamented as well as the opposite one. But a singular peculiarity attaches itself to this fault—the invitation to try the new remedy must come in a certain channel, or it will be refused; the novelty must be presented by the hands of fashion or of high caste, or it will be repulsed, whatever may be its intrinsic value. With reference to the special subject before us, another remark may be offered—the profession, by their hasty dislike and condemnation of it, have placed themselves in a false position, so that now, though they have many misgivings and surmises that it is a good thing, they are in the predicament of the fox and the grapes in Æsop's fable; when the fox found the sweet grapes were above his reach, he was fain to content himself by pronouncing them sour.

Now, Sir Benjamin, I have gathered some of these grapes, and respectfully present them to you; and though I sadly fear and sincerely regret that you are now too old to taste their sweetness, I do hope that there is chivalry enough in your venerable age to induce you to hand them over to your juniors, with a courteous expression of regard for the donor.

Let me once again remark that the difference there is between us is confined within very narrow limits; it refers only to the method of prescribing drugs. On all other subjects we are, so far as I am aware, entirely agreed. We think alike that one patient may be benefited by change of diet, a second by change of occupation, a third by travelling or change of air, a fourth by new society, a fifth by leaving off bad habits, a sixth by a surgical appliance, and that the practitioner ought to make himself familiar with all these topics, and be alive to them in consulting the welfare of his patients.

10. I will now resume the narrative of the further progress of the new method in my hands.

It is to be observed, first, that I have made no retrograde movement, that I have taken no backward step, but have endeavoured to advance a pace or two forward.

Next, that I continue to maintain the value of the suggestion that the properties of drugs should be ascertained by experiments upon the healthy; that these experiments, along with those made upon the sick, should yield the materials for a Materia Medica in which the characteristic sphere of action of each drug is discovered and described.

Next, that until this great work has been accomplished, all drugs should be given alone; otherwise the undertaking can never be finished. After this has been done, it may become lawful, and sometimes expedient, to combine two or more drugs together. A species of modified polypharmacy may possibly then be unobjectionable; but now, and for some years to come, the single medicine should be adhered to.

The principle or law of healing by drugs I am disposed to express in the two following propositions :—

I. *All drugs given in health act partially, or select certain portions or organs of the body upon which their injurious action is produced.*

II. *Drugs are to be used as remedies for diseases of the same parts or organs as those upon which they act as poisons in health.*

Or the two propositions may be combined and expressed in these words :—

Drugs select certain organs to act upon, both as poisons and as remedies, these organs being the same for each drug in both its characters, as a poison and as a remedy.

The key note of this proposition is *local action*, and the rule is that the local action shall be *on the seat of disease*.

But this proposition is only part of a more comprehensive one, which is this :—All noxious agents, the causes of diseases as well as drugs, act on the principle of selection, *e. g.*, the poison of scarlet fever selects the brain, throat, and skin, and a drug will act as a remedy in this disease if it has the power to select the same organs.

And this last proposition may be still more comprehensively stated conversely :—Those agents which *select* are noxious, those which *do not select* are salubrious and nutritive.

That contagions, or whatever generates disease, act locally, you will remember was affirmed by John Hunter. "Poisons," he says, meaning not drugs, but the causes of disease, *" take their different seats in the body as if they were allotted to them."*

While walking through pure air the body is refreshed, and health is preserved and even invigorated ; but if a miasm or infection be mixed up with a portion of the air respired, the balance of the vital powers is interfered with, and disease is the consequence. Thus, whatever destroys the equilibrium of life changes a healthy state into a morbid one.

And, again, if there are any agents at our own disposal and within our control, and drugs are such, which act locally upon those organs of the body which are already in a state of derangement or disease, these may prove to be a remedy.

Looking at health in this aspect, it is the balance of the functions of organs acting in opposing directions, the equilibrium of the vital forces of all the different parts of the body.

Here, for the present, I am arrested; observation has not taught me more, and "I affect not the pomp of superfluous"* hypotheses. Thoughts beyond the boundary line of observation, *except such as suggest further experiment*, are dreamy and fantastical; and were I to indulge in them I should soon be lost, as so many have been lost before me, in the treacherous and mis-leading by-paths of vain speculation. The witty definition given of metaphysics, "quand celui qui écoute n'entend rien, et que celui qui parle n'entend plus, c'est metaphysique," is literally true of hypothetical explanations.

But in the statements I have just made there are no hypotheses; they are statements of facts, which it may be well to repeat.

The causes of disease, so far as we are acquainted with them, act on the living body *partially*, producing their injurious effects on special organs, each having its own seat or sphere of action.

Drugs resemble these causes of disease in this, for they also act partially, one on this organ, another on that.

Drugs further resemble the causes of disease by being themselves able to produce varieties of disease very similar to those which arise from other causes.

But drugs are also remedies for disease, and the

* Sir Isaac Newton, 'Principia.'

rule for using them for this purpose is to give each
drug as a remedy in diseases of those organs upon
which it has itself a local, and, in health, an injurious
action.

I may remark further that drugs were supposed,
until recently, to act in a general manner upon the
living body; this is now denied, and local action alone
admitted. The truth is, both actions are possessed
by them; they have a general action, the tendency of
which is to depress the vital powers, and it is on this
account that, if habitually had recourse to, either in
large doses or in small ones, they seriously exhaust;
in this way, as Lord Bacon expresses it, " medicines
shorten life ;" they have also a local action, as already
explained, and the skill of the physician lies in the
wisdom with which he uses this local action in the
treatment of disease.

By the possession of both these modes of action,
general and local, drugs are characterised and distinguished from food and from stimulants; the link
which connects them with these other two classes is
formed of the substances called condiments.

But it is the local action which makes them of use
as medicines, and it is this local action in health and
in disease which ought to be the object of the physician's study.

"Formerly," says Pereira, "no distinction was
made between the effects which medicines produce
in health and those which they give rise to in
disease, and the terms *virtues, properties, faculties,* and

powers, were applied to both classes of effects. But Bichat, and subsequently Barbier and Schwilgue, pointed out the propriety of considering them separately." Here is an example of the disingenuous manner in which writers on your side adopt the views and practice of homœopathists, while they unjustly ascribe the discovery of them to others. It was Hahnemann, not Bichat, who introduced experiments in health, and charity itself will not permit us to suppose that the injustice done to Hahnemann in this sentence was inflicted in ignorance. Nevertheless, the value of provings, or experiments with drugs in health, is here not only admitted, but contended for, by this well-known authority in the Materia Medica.

As it is so difficult to you to acquire distinct notions, I repeat that the new treatment, as taught by me, is a doctrine of specifics.

That it is provided with a mode of investigation by which these specifics may be discovered in any number, and for any form of disease.

That it gives a reason for the curative action of such specifics.

Again, the specifics, the use of which is thus taught, and their method of discovery, are drugs, some of which have long been known, others have been recently discovered.

The manner in which they are discovered is by experiments made with them, first upon healthy persons, and afterwards upon sick ones. The results of the experiments on the healthy pointing out the cases in which they should be tried on the sick.

The connecting link which joins these two series of experiments together is the local action of the substances with which the experiments are made.

And the reason which this doctrine supplies for the successful treatment of sick persons by specifics is that such specifics have a local action upon the organs in which the disease exists.

11. Now, to relieve this didactic dissertation, and, I fear, wearisome repetition—wearisome, at least, to those who have not experienced the difficulty you have met with in forming distinct notions—I shall introduce a few pages from the ' Materia Medica' I have been for some time engaged upon, and give two remedies as examples of my method, and in illustration of the manner in which the doctrines I have been attempting to explain may be applied in practice. One of these drugs shall be an old one revived, the other a new one, which will, in this manner, make its entrance into the materia medica, and be presented for the first time before the medical profession, though, doubtless, should it be adopted by your party, some other name than mine will be attached to it as its discoverer.

The opportunity, for which I am thus indebted to you, also enables me to convey to my own party, through this small specimen, some notion of the plan upon which I am working ; and they can express to me, in any way that they think proper, their opinion as to the utility of such an undertaking, and whether they are disposed to encourage me to persevere with it or not.

" GOLD——AS A POISON.

" Professor Christison, quoting from Orfila, writes thus of gold:—'Its poisonous properties are powerful, and closely allied to those of the chlorides of tin and nitrate of silver. In the state of chloride it occasions death in three or four minutes when injected into the veins even in very minute doses; and the lungs are found after death so turgid as to sink in water. But if it be swallowed corrosion takes place, the salt is so rapidly decomposed that none is taken up by the absorbents, and death ensues simply from the local injury.' 'Even doses so small as the tenth of a grain have been known to produce an unpleasant degree of irritation in the stomach.' (Majendie.) 'In the state of fulminating gold this metal has given rise to alarming poisoning in former times, when it was used medicinally.' ' It excites griping, diarrhœa, vomiting, convulsions, fainting, salivation; and sometimes has proved fatal.' (Plenck.) 'Hoffmann likewise repeatedly saw it prove fatal, and the most remarkable symptoms were vomiting, great anxiety, and fainting. In one of his cases the dose (which caused death) was only six grains.' "

" Metallic gold was pulverized or triturated by the Arabians. Several modern physicians have experimented with it, thus reduced to minute subdivision, upon themselves, taking, in divided doses, one or two grains. The result of these experiments shows that gold acts upon—

" 1. The *mind* and the *brain;* producing in the former great melancholy and depression of spirits, in the latter congestion.

" 2. The *chest;* causing dyspnœa, expectoration of viscid phlegm, palpitation of the heart, congestion of the lungs.

" 3. The *digestive organs;* fetid odour from the mouth, putrid taste, salivation, nausea, flatulence, vomiting, first constipation, afterwards diarrhœa, with burning in the rectum.

" 4. The *bones,* generally, particularly the nasal, palatine, and facial bones ; giving rise to inflammation and caries.

" It is thus seen that gold has a penetrating or deep-seated action ; commencing in the brain, and affecting very specially the mind, passing through the chest and abdomen, and, finally, concentrating its energies on the bones in general, but particularly on those of the face."

" GOLD—AS A REMEDY.

" Gold was much used as a medicine some centuries ago. It was thought to promote the production of animal heat, to strengthen the heart, to restore the blood, to expel noxious humours, and particularly to exhilarate depressed spirits. For some time gold has been abandoned as a medicinal drug, it is now beginning to be employed again.

"I have prescribed triturated gold with success in the following, among other, cases :

"1. A case of extreme melancholy and despondency, arising from a Chancery suit ; the patient was in a most distressing state; after various other remedies had failed, I prescribed the first trituration (one hundredth of a grain) ; he wrote after this, 'I felt better at once.'

"2. A case of ozæna, of long standing, in which the constitution was greatly deranged, and the osseous system affected ; this boy was permanently cured.

"3. A child in a hopeless state of disease, one of the features of which was severe ophthalmia, with ulcers on the cornea in both eyes, which had resisted the prolonged and varied use of many excellent remedies ; the poor child was emaciated and exhausted with suffering and fretfulness; and the mother was almost as bad from nursing, anxiety, and want of rest. The quantity taken was a minute fraction of a grain, in divided doses. The little patient was restored, by God's blessing, to perfect health.

"4. A case of exostosis of the tibia, just below the knee, a boy; the first trituration was given with benefit ; I believe a cure was effected, but, as is often the case when that happens, the patient's friends did not think it worth while to communicate this intelligence directly to me.

" Gold is an antidote to mercury, relieving the neuralgic pains and other mischievous effects of that metal, especially when the bones have been injured by it; and, *vice versâ*, mercury is an antidote to gold.

"The organs selected by gold upon which to produce its effects are distinct, and its action profound; and, whether it be given in health or in disease, as a poison or as a remedy, the organs upon which it acts are, in both cases, the same."

The following substance has never, to my knowledge, been used in medicine before. I have proved it upon myself some years ago, and have prescribed it in a considerable number of cases, and generally with the greatest satisfaction. I have been anxious to introduce it to my professional brethren, but have hitherto kept it back, partly that I might attain a more settled confidence in it myself, and partly because I intended it to appear in its place in my own 'Materia Medica.' But as that undertaking is not yet completed, for, as may be supposed, it is one of great extent and labour; as life is uncertain; and as this opportunity seems to be a fitting one, I have much pleasure in presenting it in this place, under your auspices, Sir Benjamin, for to you it is indebted for this happy opportunity of revealing its admirable utility. I give it, not only as a specific itself, but as an illustration and proof of the value of experiments upon the healthy, as a method of discovering specifics in any number, and for any complaint; the limits to these discoveries being the very few physicians who are willing to try to make them, and the limited zeal, industry, and talent of mankind.

"TITANIUM—AS A POISON.

"Titanium was discovered by Gregor in 1791, but we are indebted to Wollaston's experiments, in 1822, for a better acquaintance with it. This rare metal is obtained chiefly from the bottom of the large smelting furnaces in iron works. Several years ago, when one of these furnaces at the Low Moor Iron Works, in Yorkshire, which had been burning without intermission for many years, was blown out for the purpose of undergoing repairs, through the kindness of Mr. Wickham, I obtained a considerable lump of titanium. The metal was in beautiful cubic crystals, of a deep-red copper colour, and very brilliant metallic lustre. I had some of these crystals triturated by the late Mr. Turner, of Manchester, and experimented with this trituration upon myself. The proportion was one grain to ninety-nine of sugar of milk. I am not aware of any other proving.

"From these experiments I am assured that titanium has a powerful action upon the human body. After taking the preparation I have described, in doses of two grains, once a day for a week, I became greatly disordered, and felt and looked wretchedly ill. On a careful consideration of my indisposition, I am justified in summing up the action of the drug as being upon—

"1. The *stomach ;* bringing on nausea, loss of appetite, and feeling of discomfort.

"2. The *brain* and *nerves ;* giddiness, imperfect vision, the peculiarity being that *half an object* only could be seen at once, desire to keep the eyelids closed.

"3. The *blood ;* a perceptible derangement of the whole system, which could not, without danger, have been carried further."

"TITANIUM—AS A REMEDY.

"I have found titanium a most valuable remedy for certain cases, for which no good remedy was known before. They are cases of degeneration of the blood. A time will come when, with a more refined chemistry, our knowledge of the constitution of the circulating fluid which is the life of man's body, and the changes it undergoes in disease, will be better understood than they are at present. We can now speak of the morbid conditions of the blood only in a crude and general manner. We know that the blood is altered from its healthy state in typhus, in chlorosis, in jaundice, in cholera, in inflammatory fever, and in some other diseases, and we can describe, in an imperfect manner, some of these changes, but there remains an inexhaustible field of research in this department of physiology and pathology. The morbid condition of the blood, which may be called the titanium condition, will be understood with some degree of accuracy by a careful study of the following case, which was the first in which it was given as a remedy.

"1. *Blood disease.*—Mr. C. F—, a middle-aged, and formerly stout and healthy man, seven years ago had an attack of typhus fever, recovered imperfectly, and has not been thoroughly well since; during the last five years has gradually but steadily become worse. He vomits a great deal, but not food; the matter rejected is a sour, watery phlegm; he has diarrhœa, the stools consisting of yellow, frothy, slimy matter; the secretion of the kidneys is high coloured and thick, (in some other cases it has been albuminous); he spits blood, and sometimes has hæmorrhage from the bowels; he has pain in the region of the liver and kidneys, and also in the lower bowels, with much cramp; the eyes slightly jaundiced; there has been great loss of strength and flesh, and two stones (twenty-eight pounds) in weight. The tongue is not much furred, and the pulse is 80. This gentleman tells me he has had a great deal of medical advice, but as yet has derived no benefit either from medicines or from careful diet, or from change of air, having during the five years paid two or three long visits at the sea-side and also one on the Welsh mountains. This account I received on the 28th of April, 1858. I prescribed half a grain of the first trituration, (one grain in a hundred), three times a day for a week, being moved

to this by the vivid recollection his narrative produced in my mind of the condition I was myself falling into while proving titanium. At the end of the
week he wrote to me that he was "altogether a different
man ;" and, without any repetition of the remedy,
and without the use of any other means, in a very
short time he regained perfect health. He continued
well a year; in the spring of 1859 he made himself
ill by hunting too much, and some of the former
symptoms showed themselves again, but they were
immediately removed by the same remedy; he has
continued generally well since."

It would extend this extract too much to give the
cases which follow; suffice it to say, that other cases,
to the number of about twelve, more or less similar
to the above, in which there was an evident breaking
up of the constitution from this special kind of de-
terioration of the blood, have been cured or greatly
benefited by this metal, given in the first or second
trituration.

The nature of the occasion which has called forth
this letter, and the urgent appeals of my publisher
for its issue, forbid that I should do more than draw
sketches of my subject. They are hastily done now,
but they are the expression of several years of labour;
I cannot be ashamed to acknowledge this when I
remember the delight with which Sir Astley Cooper
was wont to tell us that "the genius of John Hunter
was the genius of industry."

Let me add a few more sentences on the remedy, and we must then pass on to the dose.

I admit that you have the privilege of long custom on the side of your method. It was fully established by Galen, for the carrying out of his favorite hypothesis of the cardinal qualities of heat, cold, moisture, and dryness; one or more of these, he imagined, characterised all diseases, and were the *indications* for the remedies; while his *intentions* were, acting upon the principle of contraries, always to give a hot remedy for a cold disease and a dry one for a moist ailment. For the accomplishment of this purpose it was necessary that drugs should be endued with one or other of these fanciful properties. This, as you know, was the "regular" medicine for fifteen hundred years, and yet Dr. Paris, one of your brother presidents, says of it, in a lecture given before the *College of Physicians*, "it is a web of philosophic fiction which was never surpassed in absurdity."

The present "regular" practice of depletory measures on the one hand, and strengthening ones on the other—aperients and tonics—which, as a matter of fact, constitutes the routine of nine out of ten of the medical men of this country, is the modern representation of the doctrine of the ancient Methodists and of the Brunonians of later days. The *strictum* and *laxum* of the former, the *sthenic* and *asthenic* of the latter, embracing all diseases; while the corresponding characters of *relaxing* and *bracing*, or of *lowering* and *stimulating,* sums up, with convenient brevity, all the properties of all the substances applied to a therapeutic use. The injurious effects of this union of opposite extremes, as the daily guide in the treatment of the sick, have raised up many condemning voices besides those of the homœopathists, and bleeding and even purging are not nearly so popular now, as they were twenty years ago; while the other extreme is thus censured by a well-known French physician:—— " This doctrine, so seductive in its exposition, so easy in its application, is *one of the most disastrous that man has been able to imagine,* for it tends to propagate the abuse of diffusible stimulants, of which spirituous liquors make a part, an abuse excessively injurious to health in general and to the intellectual faculties in particular—an abuse to which man is naturally too much inclined, and which the sophisms of Brown have contributed to spread in all classes of English society." *

Then, again, those who decline this simple but injurious method of prescribing, run riot in all the luxuriancy of an endless polypharmacy. This is the catalogue of the properties of drugs given by Dr. Paris:——emetics, cathartics, diuretics, expectorants, diaphoretics, demulcents, antacids, absorbents, emmenagogues, refrigerants, astringents, tonics, stimulants, antispasmodics, narcotics, and anthelmintics; a somewhat shorter list than that of others before him, who added cardiacs, cephalics, carminatives, hysterics,

* Renouard, ' Histoire de la Médecine.'

agglutinants, sialogogues, stomachics, balsamics, emollients, detergents, &c. &c.

The Babel confusion of such a method is a sufficient condemnation of it, especially when you remember that the same drugs, as described by different physicians, glory in the possession of virtues not only different and opposite to, but incompatible with, each other. So that the whole system would scarcely be too harshly described as—

> "   .   .   .   fume
> Or emptiness, or fond impertinence :
> And renders us, in things that most concern,
> Unpractis'd, unprepar'd, and still to seek."*

Such being an unexaggerated picture of the actual condition of medicine, you must acknowledge that there is ample justification for any attempt to effect a reformation. Now, in the practice I advocate all the considerations just described, and which, according to your own writers, are absurd, false, and injurious, are laid aside; drugs are individually and very carefully examined, and their real physiological action ascertained by experiments made with them upon healthy persons. In this manner their sphere of action, and its character, are learned with some precision; the record is permanently attached to each drug, and becomes the guide for its use as a remedy, according to the intelligible principle I have already explained.

The treatment founded upon this method is so

* Milton, ' Paradise Lost.'

good that it rewards, by its success, all labour be-
stowed upon it; and, if generally adopted, as I trust
it will be ere long, it can afterwards fall into oblivion
from two causes only—either by being so highly
extolled as to raise unreasonable expectations, or
because it will fail, as you own your treatment does,
and as all treatment must fail, to "make men immortal."

The opposition to this treatment, at the head of
which you have placed yourself for twenty years, is
weak and foolish; this is proved by the ignorance exhibited in the arguments adduced. Your own I have
shown are quite unworthy of you, and those of others
are no better. The principal objection brought against
homœopathy by Pereira, in his gigantic work on the
materia medica, is the following :—"In many cases
homœopathic remedies would only increase the original
disease ; and we can readily imagine the ill effects
which would arise from the exhibition of acrids in
gastritis, or of cantharides in acute inflammation of
the bladder, or of mercury in salivation." Such profound ignorance as this sentence displays, in the most
learned and indefatigable writer on the materia medica
of our day, is almost incredible. Each of the examples
he gives is a case which clearly proves the truth and
value of the system he wishes to condemn by it.
Acrids are given by homœopathists in every case of
gastritis, and are admirable remedies; as for cantharides, you can scarcely find so good a remedy for
inflammation of the bladder in the whole pharmaco-

pœia; and there is none better for salivation than mercury. It would seem that the old College grudge against Dr. Groenvelt has not yet died out. You can readily *imagine* the ill effects ! While you are imagining the mischief, we are doing the good.

A short time before his melancholy death, I had some conversation with the late Dr. Baly, one of her Majesty's physicians, during the course of which he inquired, "Will opium cure apoplexy?" I answered, "Yes, if the case can be cured at all." This was a question in point, but it testified how entirely unacquainted he was with homœopathic literature and practice.

Pereira, while recommending the same drug, opium, for almost every kind of ailment, says, "In some cerebro-spinal diseases great benefit arises from the use of opium; while in other cases injury only can result from its employment; the latter effect *is to be expected* in apoplectic cases." How often has it been observed that in experimental philosophy that which was expected did not happen! So often that to say, that will happen which is least likely, has become an axiom. And if Baly and Pereira, instead of uttering an incredulous question and an ignorant surmise, had honestly set themselves to try the experiment, they would at least have placed themselves and their reputation in a more creditable position.

But the opposition to homœopathy got up by medical men is bad, not only because it is weak and foolish, but because it is not sincere. The opposition

has not respect to merits or defects in the treatment,
but to social position; it is a personal rivalry, and
betrays a conviction of the danger of being personally
supplanted.   The proof of this grave charge against a,
body of professional men, otherwise respectable, is this
—that they are eager enough to give aconite on the
recommendation of Dr. Fleming, or phosphorus on
that of Dr. Cotton, or nux vomica, or belladonna, or
any other remedy, provided some allopathic name can
be attached to it as having recommended it, while they
pretend that *the same remedies* used by homœopathists
for many years previously are useless and hurtful.
Such conduct has been characterised as " the lowest
commercial rivalry," and must bring the whole profession, and especially your section of it, into general
contempt.

You say of the present state of things, " it cannot
be helped."   I trust it may be; but if not, what
generous youth will willingly engage in a such a calling?   And what then is to hinder the profession
sinking lower and lower in the social scale?   You
speak of the "harm done to the regular profession;"
in this way it is greater than you can estimate.

12. It is painful to discuss the subject thus,
as if it were a social question.   I return to it as a
medical one with pleasure; and, as I have given you
some additional information on the principle or law
of healing by drugs, I will now tell you something
more on the matter of the *dose*, though not so much

as I could wish, my observations not being yet sufficiently advanced.

We commenced by remarking that a physician,
when consulted, has to inquire into and decide upon
three things—the nature of the patient's complaint,
the remedy most likely to do him good, and the dose
or quantity of that remedy which is required to be
taken. We have now considered the two former, and
there remains the last, the study of which forms the
science of posology.

The dose must be one *sufficient* to produce the effect
intended, that is, to answer the object for which the remedy is given; but this word "sufficient" embraces a
wide range, and involves many perplexing considerations.

Physicians have laboured to untie the intricate
twists of this Gordian knot for many centuries, but
they have not yet succeeded. Many facts have been
ascertained, but they are of a discouraging and contra-
dictory character. I will again adopt the same arrangement as before, and first give a sketch of the posology
of your party, and then a similar one of Hahnemann's.
Afterwards I will add a brief statement of my present
views upon the subject of the dose.

13. It must first be observed that it has not been
possible for you to adopt one uniform dose for all
drugs; on the contrary, a very wide difference exists
between the quantity sufficient for a dose of one drug
and that enough for a dose of another drug. "The

doses," says Dr. Paris, " of medicinal substances are specific with respect to each." This at once creates a great difficulty.

Again, the same drug acts differently in different quantities; of some drugs larger doses produce a more powerful effect than smaller ones; on the contrary, with other drugs the action is increased by diminishing the quantity. " 'The young and eager practitioner," says the authority just quoted, " is too often betrayed into the error of supposing that the powers of a remedy always increase in an equal ratio with its dose." Did you, Sir Benjamin, wish us to consider you a young and eager practitioner when you ignored this well-known fact, and indulged in the following satire?—" Hitherto it had been supposed that the effects of any medicinal substance taken into the system bear some proportion to the quantity taken; that if two mercurial pills taken daily would make the gums sore, four would make them very sore." (' Quarterly Review.')

Again, of drugs in a solid state, some act in proportion to the quantity taken, but others, the common metals, for example (see Christison), are *inert* in the crude form, that is, in a state of mechanical aggregation, whereas the same substances, triturated or finely pulverized by rubbing, act powerfully in very small quantities; a pound of mercury may be swallowed without medicinal action, while two or three grains, after trituration, will act strongly.

And again, of drugs in a state of solution, some

7

act more or less energetically in proportion to the quantity, while with others smaller doses, largely diluted, exhibit more power than larger ones given in a more concentrated form. In general, solution increases the action of drugs, as trituration does.

The continued repetition of the same dose of some drugs produces a cumulative or increasing effect; on the other hand, with other drugs, the effects of the first doses diminish or wear out.

Such are the principal facts or conclusions hitherto ascertained in your school; it will be seen that they rather exhibit the uncertainty, difficulty, and confusion of the subject, than its elucidation.

The object for which you prescribe drugs is, in general, to produce certain specified effects, such as evacuation of the stomach, perspiration, &c., and the doses of the drugs given for these purposes must be strong enough to produce these intended results. They are therefore necessarily *large*, often as large as if they were given to produce the poisonous effects of the drug in health.

The only exception to this rule is in the case of drugs given under the significant name of " alteratives." Of these the dose is generally smaller. If the drug so given happens to be the specific remedy for the complaint for which it is prescribed, it is the adoption of the practice of our school; if it is not specific, more harm than good will result from its administration.

Need I repeat the remark that medication, in this

gross form, must be injurious to that very large proportion of sick persons who, according to your letter, would recover with "no treatment at all"? And for those who cannot so recover it is, at the best, but a very indirect method of assisting them.

If to these difficulties of the dose in the old school be added those arising from the adulteration of the drugs; the mistakes and carelessness in their preparation; the interference of one drug with another, when several are mixed together in one prescription; and the fact that they are often thrown away by the patient instead of being taken by him as prescribed, it may be, in some degree, understood that the task of unravelling such a knot is hopeless.

You have no rule to guide you in the choice of remedies; you can have none for the selection of the dose, except the old one, so full of humour, "let it be done *secundum artem !*"

14. We now turn to the members of the new school, and desire to learn how it stands with them in the matter of the dose. We have seen that they have a rule for the selection of the remedy, and that the object for which drugs are given by them is very different from yours, namely, that it is to act upon, not the healthy, but the diseased organs; it follows from this, as a necessary consequence, that the doses must be *small*. Beyond this general point of agreement, however, there is nothing settled as yet; as with you, it is a matter of experience, and consequently,

as with you, every practitioner is left to form an experience for himself, and he is to be guided by that.

Hahnemann began with ordinary doses, but was compelled to reduce these by the mischief frequently done by them. Having gone from less to less, and, to his amazement, still finding effects follow his dose, the novelty and surprise overpowered his judgment, and in his old age he issued the decree that the best dose for all diseases, whether acute or chronic, was the smallest quantity of the thirtieth dilution. As far as I can learn, however, he did not adhere to this unwise dictum himself, nor have I heard of any homœopathist after him who has done so.

Nearly all practitioners make use of a considerable variety in the dilutions and triturations they select for doses.

Some confine themselves very much to the higher dilutions or smaller doses, others to the lower or stronger ones, while a few prescribe the original preparations, or, as they are called, the mother tinctures.

In the earlier days of homœopathy it was thought best by some to prefer the higher dilutions as especially adapted for acute disease of short standing, and the lower ones for chronic or long-lasting ailments.

At the present time the contrary opinion prevails, and the lower preparations are given in acute cases, and the higher in chronic ones.

All which fluctuations must continue to prevail, as they do in your school, so long as, in both cases, the subject is one of personal experience only.

15. A question of great interest, therefore, arises —Can any law or principle for the selection of the dose be discovered, as there has been for the remedy?

The earlier homœopathic writers answer this inquiry by a direct negative ; one says, " it is, in fact, altogether impossible to lay down any precise rules as to the dose." This reminds one of the language used by Dr. Paris as to a similar impossibility of discovering a rule for the choice of the remedy.

Later authorities are pretty much of the same way of thinking. When the subject was last discussed, a few years ago, one physician remarked that he " did not believe that a law as to the dilution could ever be arrived at ;" another " feared a law relating to the dilution could not be established, experience being the only sure guide in this matter." But, as we have seen, experience is not a sure guide, and I marvel that, when one difficulty has been overcome in respect to the drug, the remaining difficulty with respect to the dose should be considered invincible.

The truth is, that so long as physicians looked only in the direction of the disease and the patient, Sydenham's earnest wish for the possession of a " fixed, definite, and consummate method of healing " could not be attained, though pursued for many centuries ;

and in like manner, while the attention of practitioners is directed only to the same objects, the possession of a fixed rule for the dose will be equally unattainable. But no sooner was the direction changed, and the thinking mind turned towards the drug as well as towards the disease, than the first law of healing was laid hold of, imperfectly, indeed, at that time, but so as to admit of more distinct and accurate definition now. And, in like manner, if we tread in the same steps, if we look in the same direction, that is, if we examine the drug with more care and precision, we shall find the law of the dose. It is the counterpart of the law of the remedy, as stated in this letter, is dependent upon the *relation* which exists between the dose or quantity of a drug and the disease connected with it, and may be expressed provisionally in these words :—

Different doses of the same drug, given in health, select different organs on which to act injuriously.

Corresponding, but smaller, doses of the same drug are to be given as remedies in the diseases of the organs which they select.

The key-note, as was observed in the law of the drug, is *local action*, and belongs to the relation which ties together the dose and the organ.

You will not be interested in, nor is this the place

to give detailed illustrations of this rule ; I must content myself with adducing one drug as an example,
and with adding two or three remarks.

Oxalic acid :—this drug, as a poison, acts in the
largest doses upon the *alimentary canal ;* in smaller
ones, upon the *heart ;* in still smaller, upon the *spinal
cord ;* and in the smallest, upon the *brain.* The effects
of the concentrated acid are to inflame and corrode
the stomach ; the other effects are thus described by
Professor Christison :—" When considerably diluted,
the phenomena are totally different. When dissolved in
twenty parts of water, oxalic acid ceases to corrode,
nay it hardly even irritates, but it causes death by
acting on the brain, spine, or heart, the symptoms
varying with the dose. When the quantity is large,
the most prominent symptoms are those of palsy of
the heart. When the dose is less, the animal perishes
after several fits of violent tetanus, which affect the
respiratory muscles of the chest in particular, causing
spasmodic fixing of the chest and consequent suffo-
cation. When the dose is still less, the spasms are
slight or altogether wanting, and death occurs under
symptoms of pure narcotism, like those caused by
opium ; the animal appears to sleep away. The
poison produces nearly the same effects to whatever
texture of the body it is applied."

According to the rule just expressed, this drug must
be given in corresponding but smaller doses as a
remedy. If for an affection of the brain, the dose
must be the smallest which will produce any effect ;

if for one of the spine, a somewhat larger dose will be required ; if for a disease of the heart, the dose is to be still further increased.

Other examples might easily be given, but I must forbear. Of course our knowledge on the subject must be, at present, necessarily very imperfect, but labour will improve this, if only it is directed in the proper channel.

Of many drugs it will be objected that we know no such distinction as is here indicated in the selection made by different doses ; the reply to this objection is, that until such distinctions are made out there is no sufficient reason for varying the dose.

Much has been said on the different susceptibility of different patients to the action of remedies, and it has been argued that the dose must vary according to this. I am of opinion that this difference has been much exaggerated, and that if the right remedy is really known, the dose need vary little on this account.

A dose may be known to be sufficient in two ways —first, by curing the complaint ; and secondly, by producing some of the effects known to belong to the drug ; this last may happen either along with the cure of the ailment or without it ; if without it, the remedy should be immediately discontinued, as an improper one.

I need scarcely say that I have no sympathy with those who talk of dividing a globule into halves and quarters, nor much with those who use globules at all; at the same time I cannot but condemn in the strongest manner the wicked sneers and sarcasms which some of the opponents of homœopathy have indulged in with respect to them.

I will not at present venture to add more on this difficult and intricate subject; but if it please God we live a few years longer, and you should write another letter in 'Fraser,' I shall hope to have something more to tell you in reply.

IV.

1. In the concluding part of your letter you enter upon the subject of State medicine, and the conduct of the authorities towards the profession and towards the public in affairs relating to health.

This affords me both the opportunity and the justification, which you cannot blame me for availing myself of, for inviting the attention of Her Majesty's Government, Parliament, and the British nation, to the manner in which power was first sought, and, when this could not be obtained, license has been since taken by the medical colleges to oppose the progress of medical reformation.

2. In the month of June, 1855, a Medical Bill was introduced into the House of Commons, read a first time, and ordered to be printed for the purpose of circulation and discussion during the recess. The preamble stated that "it is expedient to amend the laws relating to the medical profession," and the Bill provided for a Medical Council and a general

registration of qualified men, and defined the privileges of the faculty thus registered. I read the Bill
at the time, and saw no reason why I should take any
part either for or against it.

In February, 1856, at the beginning of the following session, this Bill was reintroduced into the House
of Commons, and read a first time. On this occasion
the Premier (Lord Palmerston) is reported to have
said that the Bill had met with so little opposition
from the profession that it should have the support
of the Government. In a few days it was read a
second time, and ordered to be committed in a week.
It was not till this stage of its progress that I saw it,
nor was I anxious to see it, supposing it to be a re-
production, in all fairness, of the model Bill. I now
read it, however, and to my intense surprise I found
the following clause introduced, not a word of which
existed in the Bill of 1855, and about which nothing
whatever had been said in the House.

"XXIX. If any of the said several colleges shall
at any time *strike off* from the list of such college the
name of any one of their members *who has been guilty
of misconduct*, such college shall signify to the Medical Registrar the name of the member so struck off,
and the Medical Registrar *shall erase forthwith such
name from the Register*, and shall not restore such
name," &c.

This was revealing an object, and introducing an
element altogether so new and different from the apparent purpose of the model Bill, that I felt it impera-

tive to do what I could to frustrate the clandestine effort; for, were such a clause to become law, I knew well that there would be no greater "misconduct" in the eyes of the medical colleges, than the adoption of homœopathy; and that no names would be so quickly "struck off" as those of the members who had seen it to be their duty to embrace this mode of practice.

I, therefore, immediately went to London, and along with three medical colleagues, Dr. M. J. Chapman, Dr. J. Hodgson Ramsbotham, and Dr. J. B. Metcalfe, sought an interview with the honorable member, (Mr. Headlam,) who had charge of the Bill. We explained the probable operation of the "striking off" clause, Mr. Headlam was not easily convinced that it could be turned to such a persecuting purpose as we believed; but when he did see it, he said that rather than carry such a clause he would give up the Bill, and readily assented to move in Committee the following addition to it :—" Provided always that any differences of opinion on the theory or practice of medicine or surgery shall not be construed into *misconduct.*"

When the day for the committee arrived, the Secretary of State (Sir George Grey) moved several amendments. The mover of the Bill complained of this, and in justification, the Secretary of State explained that the College of Physicians had waited on him only *the day before,* to request him to do this for them. Some confusion arose, and the Bill was referred to a select committee.

It would be tedious to pursue the details of the struggle which followed; but, during the sessions of 1856, 1857, and 1858, a rapid succession of amended medical bills was printed, in which this proviso was alternately omitted and inserted, as the college or myself happened to prevail.

On the 2nd of August, 1858, the Bill became an Act, and the clause, considerably modified, and with the proviso, which had become altered in expression, but not in meaning, attached, became law.

Another, but a shorter, effort was made by other homœopathic practitioners, for the introduction of a clause for the protection of medical students; this was also successfully incorporated into the Act in the House of Lords.

3. The law upon these two subjects is now contained and expressed in the two following clauses of the Medical Act :—

"XXVIII. If any of the said colleges or the said bodies at any time exercise any power they possess by law of striking off from the list of such college or body the name of any one of their members, such college or body shall signify to the General Council the name of the member so struck off; and the General Council may, if they see fit, direct the registrar to erase forthwith from the Register the qualification derived from such college or body in respect of which such member was registered, and the Registrar shall note the same therein : Provided always that the name of no person shall be erased from the Register on the ground of his having adopted any theory of medicine or surgery."

This clause protects homœopathic practitioners ; the following was intended for the protection of students inclined to adopt homœopathic practice :—

" XXIII.   In case it shall appear to the General Council that an attempt has been made by any body, entitled under this Act to grant qualifications, to impose upon any candidate offering himself for examination an obligation to adopt or refrain from adopting the practice of any particular theory of medicine or surgery, as a test or condition of admitting him to examination or of granting a certificate, it shall be lawful for the said Council to represent the same to Her Majesty's most honorable Privy Council, and the said Privy Council may thereupon issue an injunction to such body so acting, directing them to desist from such practice ; and in the event of their not complying therewith, then to order that such body shall cease to have the power of conferring any right to be registered under this Act so long as they shall continue such practice."

4. Such was the successful issue of the struggle in Parliament, and such is now the law of the land. But how has the law been obeyed ?   Among other breaches of it, take the following resolutions of two of the medical colleges as examples.

At a meeting of the Council of the Royal College

of Surgeons in Ireland, held in August, 1861, it was ordained that—

"No fellow or licentiate of the college shall pretend or profess to cure diseases by the deception called homœopathy, or the practice called mesmerism, or by any other form of quackery. * * * It is also hereby ordained that no fellow or licentiate of the college shall consult with, meet, advise, direct, or assist any person engaged in such deceptions or practices, or in any system or practice considered derogatory or dishonorable by physicians and surgeons."

Is not this an illegal by-law? Is it not in direct contravention of the Act of Parliament? Certainly, whatever lawyers may make of the letter, it is directly in opposition to the spirit and intention of the legislature; it is an act of tyranny, betrays great bigotry and improper feeling, and calls for the interference of some power to compel its withdrawal.

To the same effect the Irish College of Physicians has adopted the following form of declaration to be taken by licentiates on admission :—

" I engage not to practise any system or method (so called) for the cure or alleviation of disease, *of which the college has disapproved.* (!) * * * and in case of any doubt relative to the true meaning or application of this engagement, I *promise to submit* to the judgment of the college. And I solemnly and sincerely declare, that should I violate any of the conditions specified in this declaration, so long as I shall be either a licentiate or fellow of the college, I shall render myself liable, and *shall submit*, to censure of the college, pecuniary fine (not exceeding twenty pounds), or *expulsion and surrendering of the diploma, which-ever the president and fellows of the college, or the majority of them, shall think proper to inflict.*"

It is difficult to believe that men of intelligent minds and upright moral principles can enter the college on such humiliating terms. This again, therefore, must deteriorate the profession, lower the standard of character of its members, and her Majesty and her subjects must receive "great damage and hurt" thereby.

Such unconstitutional and, as it would appear, illegal proceedings as these demand the exercise of a restraining and controlling power; the twenty-third clause of the Medical Act intimates the existence of such a power; and it is to be hoped that some members, either of the Government or of Parliament, will exert themselves to bring this power into opera-tion, so that the liberty of professional and scientific investigation *by qualified men*, intended to be guaran-teed by the Sovereign and the Legislature in this Act of Parliament, may be effectually and practically se-cured to them.

The medical profession is a commonwealth, and cannot, with justice or safety to the national welfare, be subjected to despotic government within itself. All its members, when once called to its duties, are on an equal footing; and though it is needful that a dozen individuals be chosen to regulate the education

and secure the fitness of candidates, and to admit
them when so fitted, these individuals are in no way
qualified or entitled to hamper or victimise thought
and experiment in medical science. I hope, Sir Benjamin, this is a very distinct notion, and that our gra-
cious Sovereign and her whole people will be able to
perceive its force and act upon its requirements, and
so secure, to all members of the medical faculty alike,
that freedom in the pursuit of their professional duties,
without which the nation cannot be duly and faithfully served, in the matter of health and life.

In addition to this freedom for thought and inquiry,
which ought to be granted to and exercised by all
qualified men equally, there are two other points of
importance in this subject on which it is necessary to
have "very distinct notions."

They are so well expressed by Mr. Rumsey, of Chel-
tenham, in his 'Essays on State Medicine,' published
in 1856, that I cannot do better than adopt his words.

"A weighty hindrance to legislation," this gentleman observes, "has consisted in the indifference of
the majority of the profession to any measure which
would not guarantee to them a monopoly of curative
practice. Their cry is 'protection.'*   *   *   *
They require that none should be admitted into
the ranks of the profession except those adhering to
'orthodox' medical theories and authorised modes of
practice.

" Now it cannot be denied that improvements in
medical science, of great benefit to mankind, have now

and then originated externally to the pale of the 'regular' faculty, whilst many of those still more important reforms and discoveries, made within that pale, have been vehemently opposed, and the progress of truth for a time checked, by the heads and governing councils of the profession.

" Any medical doctrine not sanctioned by those authorities has accordingly been accounted heterodox, and no discreet aspirant for medical honours has ventured to consider it even an open question.
*　*　*

" The prohibition sought for would not apply specially to uneducated medicine-vendors, who, notwithstanding their entire ignorance of the merest elements of pharmacy and therapeutics, profess, without legal hindrance, to furnish infallible remedies for every ailment.　*　*　*

" But on the protective hypothesis most in favour with the medical profession, what would become of certain *legally qualified practitioners* who forsake the beaten path, as, for example, the disciples of Hahnemann?　*　*　*

" Let any of these—more especially if highly educated or keen witted, most certainly if skilful or successful—be found in the nominal ranks of the medical profession, and they would inevitably be expelled, forbidden to exercise their occupation, probably punished severely.　*　*　*

" It appears that there are two very distinct demands :—

" First. That no one should be legally authorised to practise medicine who does not avow that he is prepared to treat disease on principles and precedents approved by the most eminent professors and practitioners of the day; in other words, on the therapeutical systems sanctioned by the heads of the medical colleges.

" Secondly. That the state should grant its licence to practise medicine to those only (1) whose knowledge of anatomy, physiology, and pathology, and of the various branches of abstract and natural science, on which philosophical medicine rests, has been duly tested; (2) who can produce evidence, by certificates fairly earned and fairly granted, of having carefully observed by clinical attendance, enough of the medical systems now in force, and who have sufficiently studied the history of those in past ages to preserve them from ignorant, precipitate, and fallacious conclusions; (3) whose preliminary education has been sound and liberal, and whose character, disposition, and habits are such as to fit them alike for the sterner requirements and the more scrupulous proprieties of their calling.

" One of these demands, it will be at once perceived, is for professional protection against irregularity, heterodoxy, and intrusion.

" The other is for public protection against ignorance, incompetence, and, what is worst of all, a low standard of professional morality.

" Now I do not hesitate to assume that the second only of these demands would be acceded to by an enlightened government.

" A law carrying protection to this extent, and no
further, is so essential an item of public health protection, that it can no longer be neglected in this
country, with just regard to the safety of its inhabi-
tants " For many other sensible remarks and sug-
gestions on medical education and sanitary measures,
I am glad of the opportunity of referring to this book.

As you have set me the example of quoting yourself, I venture to repeat some observations made by
me in a review of Mr. Rumsey's essays in a medical
journal published at the time (1856). This must
close what I have to say at present on state medicine.

The truth upon this important subject seems to be
contained in the following propositions :—

1. The Sovereign, viewed in the patriarchal or
parental character, will necessarily take an active part
in the care of the people, when suffering from bodily
disease.

2. The state, therefore, will use *preventive* measures, directing its attention to everything calculated
to promote the sanitary or healthy condition of the
people, and to ward off disease.

3. The state will also provide the best means of
cure. This implies the providing and supervision of
a medical profession—physicians, accoucheurs, and
surgeons—also of drugs and druggists, nurses, medicines, and hospitals.

4. The provision of medical attendants on the sick
implies a *suitable education*, a *state licence*, and a
sphere of duty.

5. The *education* of men to be engaged in so important a duty implies a provision by the state of a preliminary liberal school and university training, and a subsequent professional one.

6. The *licence* to practise implies examination as to competency and to character, and is a certificate to that effect.

7. This examination ought to extend only to the subject matter of the previous education, to the talents, acquirements, and moral character of the candidate. It ought not to fetter the future progress of thought or inquiry, nor exact any pledge except that of a conscientious discharge of the duty undertaken towards rich and poor, with integrity, humanity, and good morals. These examinations should be public, as they are for degrees in our universities.

8. The protection afforded by this state licence is not, and ought not to be, a protection of the profession in favour of any exclusive, speculative, or practical orthodoxy, or in favour of the heads of colleges and their private friends and personal supporters, and against those who, while equally well educated, and possessing the same legal qualification, differ in matters of opinion and practice, and have not the same court influence; such a protection cannot fail to be inquisitorial and tyrannical, and must greatly impede scientific progress and practical improvement; it would also exceed the object desired by a parental government, and cripple the just liberty of the subject.

9. The protection the state wishes to supply is the protection of its people from ignorance, incompetency, fraud, and immorality.

10. It is in order to supply *this* protection that the state should interfere and provide suitable education, and give a testimonial or licence.

11. For this object the state should establish by law an appropriate machinery in teachers, professors, and examiners; all of whom, while left free in the intelligent pursuit of their professional studies, would be the servants of the state, and under its supervision as to the efficient discharge of their respective duties.

12. A *sphere of duty* implies that the state should seek to regulate the supply by the demand, so as to prevent the mischief which would otherwise arise from an overstocked and impoverished profession.

Such are the considerations which, as it appears to me, should engage the grave attention and stimulate the active efforts of a paternal government with reference to the sick among its people.

The sick and suffering are always to be found, and claim the care of the community of which they form a large proportion.

The state must care for these, and protect them by providing that means of succour be within their reach.

On the other hand, the medical attendant needs some sympathy, care, and protection also; he is not to be overborne, nor taken advantage of, nor blamed when unreasonable expectations cannot be fulfilled, when pain continues, disease advances, and life ebbs away, notwithstanding his most anxious and best directed efforts.

Sometimes, indeed, pain and disease are aggravated, and death is hastened, by unskilful treatment ; but more frequently pain is relieved, disease arrested or removed, and life prolonged by the blessing of God on the knowledge, skill, and care of the physician.

Such knowledge and skill are acquired with difficulty and pain ; the care needful in the use of them often calls for self-denial, and is attended with much labour, and sometimes with suffering. The office of the physician is, therefore, a worthy post, and the faithful performance of its duties gives him a claim upon his Sovereign for countenance, and upon his fellow-subjects for grateful respect.

5. Another topic akin to the one we have just now discussed is the question whether the homœo-pathists shall be constituted a separate medical body. On your side, there has been a great effort to compel them to take this step, and, on their side, there has existed a considerable desire for the accomplishment of such a separation. This was a natural consequence of the mutual animosity. In America the separation has been effected, and there are now homœopathic universities at Philadelphia, at Cleveland in Ohio, and at New York, charged by the government with the same duties, and in all respects possessing the same privileges and position as the older allopathic universities. There are, I am informed, about three

thousand practitioners of this school in the different states.

But shall it be done in England? I hope not; I think it would be unwise; and whenever the subject has been discussed, during the last twelve years, I have used what influence I might have, to dissuade homœopathists from making the attempt. And for these reaosns :—

The separation would constitute two rival sects, and perpetuate the opposition and enmity indefinitely, and there would be no hope of either party convincing or silencing the other.

By waiting and ventilating the subject, and especially by the exhibition of a better spirit, which ought not to be despaired of, the truth will gradually insinuate itself, even into the most exclusive and bigoted seats of authority; and so the reformation in medicine will become general and national, and the universities, colleges, schools, and hospitals remain united as at present. In spite of all the outward manifestations of hostility, a great amelioration of general practice, through the unwelcome influence of homœopathy, has already been brought about; and, if Plato is right when he says " τὸ γάς ἀληθὲς οὐδέποτε ἐλέγχεται," truth is never refuted or vanquished, the accomplishment of the happy result may be confidently expected.

Suppose the separation effected, and the homœopathists by Royal Charter, or by Act of Parliament, constituted an independent faculty of medicine, why should not every new opinion, and every modification of practice, which may arise within the profession, claim a similar privilege? If, instead of adopting and incorporating what is good in each, a process of propagation by slips is to be adopted, where is it to end?

And, for your side of the fence, Sir Benjamin, neither would it be less unwise, for, as it is not for the good of the public to be without a profession, so neither would it be for the good of the profession to detach from it a portion of its members. You cannot amputate a limb without mutilating the body.

Other reasons might be added, but these are abundantly sufficient, I think, to satisfy reasonable and unambitious persons that it is best to bear the inconveniences of the present transition state, great though they undoubtedly are, than plunge into the difficulties and distractions which would necessarily accompany the division of a profession which should always remain a united body.

6. Then, if we are to remain united, what is to become of the exhibition of childish temper on the subject of consultations? The Dublin College condescends to forbid medical men of different views to meet, and you have written thus :—

" To join with homœopathists in attendance on cases of either medical or surgical disease would be neither wise nor honest. The object of a medical consultation is the good of the patient ; and we cannot suppose that any such result can arise from the interchange of opinions where the views entertained, or *professed to be entertained*, (!) by one of the parties as to the nature and treatment of disease are wholly unintelligible to the other." Or, as you touch the tender point in another letter :—

" I do not think that any well-educated medical practitioner can honestly meet *one of these* homœopathists in consultation. The only object of a consultation is to do good to the patient; and it is out of the question to suppose that any interchange of ideas with one in whose *professed* opinions we have not the smallest faith, and whose notions, indeed, we cannot comprehend, can tend to this result."

Now, the bitter animus displayed in these sentences will not escape the notice of the most casual general reader; and I do not think it unbecoming in me to rebuke you for it. I have heard that your letter has been called "a crushing letter" by one of your supporters. It has not crushed me, and, as it did not crush homœopathy twenty years ago, it is not likely to crush it now; shall I tell you what it will injure? Your fair fame, your reputation in the next generations, these, I am sorry to believe, will be tarnished by the unworthy part you have acted in this controversy.

But you ask, "Why are we to meet?" I will tell you; because the patient, a suffering fellow-creature, wishes it. But you somewhat impatiently exclaim, "What good can arise?" I will tell you again; more to your side than to ours, besides the patient's satisfaction. It is the patient, not I, who requests the consultation; it is you who are afraid, not I, of the meeting. Why? Because in this way we make converts. And it may as well be told that all the anathemas of all the colleges will not prevent such meetings. Not long ago I was visiting a lady at some distance, and she asked my leave to send for her ordinary medical adviser, that I might tell him my opinion of her case, which I willingly consented to do. When he came, I warned him of the risk he run in seeing my face in opposition to the resolutions of his professional brethren; his manly answer was, "But I will if I like!" This will serve for a rebuke for Mr. Fergusson; and it is by no means a solitary proof that Britons do not yet intend to be made slaves.

But I earnestly desire not to be overcome by provocation to write unadvisedly, and I wish to tell you further of the good that may arise from consultations— there can be an interchange of thought; there can be a friendly recognition, and mutual courtesies; there may be mutual instruction; and men thus brought together may learn to respect each other, who, but for such a meeting, might have learned only to disparage and to despise each other. The late Mr. Babington and I met in this manner, I believe with comfort and pleasure on both sides, and why may not others do the same?

In thus advocating an occasional interview between medical men of the two schools, I am not to be misunderstood or misrepresented as seeking this as a matter of help, countenance, or benefit to the homœo-pathic party ; this body is quite competent to manage its own cases, and is not dependent upon aid from your side. The opportunities which offer for such meetings arise out of the circumstances in which homœopathists are occasionally placed, and they are these two—the scattered and isolated position of some practitioners, who are, perhaps, many miles distant from their nearest colleague, who could help them were he accessible ; but not being so, and the nature of the case rendering the presence of a second medi-cal man unavoidable, it becomes necessary to ask the help of an allopathic neighbour. This circumstance is not common, but it happens sometimes ; it belongs to the department of the accoucheur or the surgeon almost exclusively.

The other circumstance is more common, and occurs when a homœopathist is sent for to see a patient fifty or a hundred miles off; it may be a case of dangerous acute disease, and there is no homœopathist near at hand ; or a chronic case, which has been long in the hands of some favorite and well-known medical friend. The acute case ought to be seen daily, but the distance makes this impos-sible, and the friends of the patient remark that it would be a comfort to them if their usual medical attendant may be asked to meet the homœopathist, and come, from time to time, in the intervals between his visits ; they may thus learn from the allopathic attendant how the case is going on, and their anxiety be somewhat relieved. There is nothing unreasonable or unprofessional in such a course ; it differs little from other distant consultation visits ; it is a position of affairs which has frequently happened to myself, and I have much pleasure in testifying to the readiness and courtesy with which, in general, such a service has been rendered. I am always frank ; I say to my medical brother when he arrives, " I am glad to see you ; I hope we shall agree in our diagnosis and views as to the general management of the case ; and with regard to the drugs which may be required, I shall explain to you what I wish to prescribe ; you will thus have an excellent opportunity of witnessing and watching the results of homœopathic treatment, without the responsibility of a first trial made by yourself. I have nothing to conceal, and you have only to act honorably, of course making no attempt to undermine the confidence of the patient or his friends during my absence." The attendance continues, in acute cases, perhaps a few weeks, in chronic ones for months or even a year or two, and ends with feelings of mutual respect. Why should such meetings be interfered with or prevented ? It is for the public to see to it that they are not deprived of such a benefit ; they have the power to do so, if they are willing to exert it.

I have alluded to Mr. Fergusson. The call made upon him was for a consultation visit to render surgical assistance ; it belongs, therefore, to the first of the two circumstances I have now described. I think it fitting his letters should be preserved, and you will find them in the Appendix along with your own. The awkward corner he has placed himself in may operate as a warning to others, and lead to the exercise of more moral courage, and the exhibition of more creditable conduct.

7. When the subject of state medicine is under consideration it is impossible to overlook that section of it which relates to the arbitrary and tyrannical conduct of individual medical men placed in posts of public duty. Among other departments, this is often conspicuous in the army, and needs to be restrained by exposure, and by bringing to bear upon it the force of public opinion. I cannot describe the workings of professional prejudice, in positions of authority, better than it has been done in the ingenuous and lively autobiographical sketch given us by the late Dr. William Fergusson, Inspector-General of Military Hospitals; whether any relative of the gentleman I have just named, I do not know.

"Until our experience in the Peninsular war, there had been but one opinion amongst us of the utter incurability of the disease but by mercury, and if, through chance, the disease got well without it, we had as little hesitation in declaring that it could not possibly have been the disease, but some other putting on that form. In short, there was one specific, which was mercury, and that was to be administered, at all hazards, to all the afflicted, no matter what may have been the patient's capability of bearing the remedy, the nature of his constitution, or the sufferings it entailed. Things were in this state at the beginning of the present century, when, during the year of the peace of Amiens, I was made to accompany the late Duke of Gloucester in a tour to the north of Europe, during which we chanced to arrive at Moscow when a contest was raging between the pro- and anti-mercurialists of the faculty for the appointment to an hospital that had just been founded by one of the Prince Gallitzins. His excellency, an enlightened man, was sufficiently inclined to the first, but, before deciding, did me the honour to consult me on the occasion. I need not say to what side I inclined, or how much I wondered at what appeared to me the barbarous ignorance of the people where such a question could have been raised. I set it down, however, as one of the strange things a passing traveller often hears of, but has neither time to investigate nor understand.

"Two or three years after this, when I was doing duty in the home district, on my promotion to be Deputy-Inspector of Hospitals, and it became my business to examine the weekly returns of the regiments in England at the Medical Board Office, we were utterly astonished on its being reported that more than one surgeon of the King's German Legion were infected with the same heresy as the non-mercurialists of Moscow! and they promptly met the treatment of heretics. *Instant retraction, or expulsion from service, was the alternative.*

" I certainly never expected to hear more of what appeared to me so strange and pernicious a delusion; but on my appointment to be chief of the Medical Department to the Portuguese Auxiliary Army in the Peninsula, in the year 1810, I found that the native faculty never used mercury, or very little if any, and they obstinately contended for the right and propriety of their practice. Such infatuation, as I then thought it, *was not to be reasoned with.* I applied to the Commander-in-Chief, and obtained *the strongest general order that could be penned,* ordaining the use of mercury.

" Still I was beat. Wherever I could not personally superintend, the remedy was neglected; if present, the mercury was neutralized with sulphur; and when I insisted upon seeing whether it had been rubbed in, was presented with a skin as black as an Ethiop's. At first their dislike and horror for the remedy was so great that they would rush from the room when it was applied, and wash it off with soap and water. In fact, I saw that I was playing a losing game where I could not help myself, [I hope you will see this is your case, Sir Benjamin,] yet at the same time I could not help acknowledging that the grave consequences I apprehended must have ensued from their preposterous conduct *did not follow,* and that our soldiers, who were mercurialized I may say to extremity, *often suffered them in the most lamentable degree.* [This is just what you should acknowledge, in our present controversy.]

"Things went on in this way for about two years longer, when I was despatched to Evora, in the Alentego, to take charge of the medical department, where I found a large hospital under excellent management, by far the best I had ever seen in Portugal, and the list of cases amounted to nearly fifty, all of them severe, and all doing well, without ever having taken a particle of mercury, which had never been used amongst them from time immemorial. I had been, meanwhile, in the *constant habit of inquiring* amongst *and observing* our own soldiers, and when I compared the difference of their condition, full of mercury, with that of the native troops, who never took a particle, I cannot describe the astonishment it raised. [This is what you ought to have done in our case; had you inquired and observed in the same honest manner, your astonishment would not have been less.] Still I could not bring myself to believe that I had *lived so long in utter error,* and I wrote from the spot the first English essay that had appeared in our times, of the curability of the disease without mercury *amongst the Portuguese,* for I durst not at first *open my eyes* to the whole truth; and within two years afterwards, first Mr. Rose, and then Mr. Guthrie, ventured upon bolder views, and published to the world the feasibility, propriety, and safety of

9

treating British soldiers in the same manner as the Portuguese.

" I confess that nothing in the practice of physic ever staggered me more than this discovery—*that the creed of ages should be found utterly baseless*—that *the wisest amongst us* should have, in all the intermediate time, been destroying instead of saving their patients, by murderous and unnecessary courses of mercury—was enough to shake the firmest faith in physic, and to prove that what might seem the best established principles of medicine were no more than the delusion of the passing day. * * * This stumbling-block (a course of mercury) we ourselves had set up, misled the philosophic Abernethy. He, believing in the incurability without mercury, was utterly confounded when he saw some of the worst cases yield as if by magic to some of the simplest mercurial alteratives, which he had administered as *preliminary* to the established course. [You might have sometimes witnessed such speedy cures of other complaints if you had tried our method.] He inquired amongst the best surgeons of his own school, who assured him that the cases *could not be* what he took them for. To be sure, they looked like it ; but, *as they got well in the way they did they must be something else,* and he therefore wrote his work on pseudo-diseases. A stronger instance of the tenacity of the human mind in adherence to error never was exhibited. [Perhaps, Sir Benjamin, you have surpassed Mr. Abernethy now.] He was a philosopher, but he could not forego the prejudices that had been instilled into his mind in early life; and, rather than open his eyes to the truth, he chose *to invent an imaginary order of diseases*, which, *had he allowed to be real*, must have held up a mirror to his view, which he could not have looked into without owning that he had all his life been destroying in many instances, instead of curing his patients. * * * Amidst all this blundering and prejudice, it seems never to have been discovered that mercury was, after all, making its own work, *by producing the very appearances it was given to eradicate;* for so like are the abrasions of the mouth and throat, or other secreting surfaces, resulting from mercury and from disease, that the best experienced cannot, even now, distinguish between them; and in former times went on destroying in the dark, always believing, while their patients were falling before their eyes, that their practice was orthodox and indisputable."*

Such is the language, not of a homœopathist, but of the late Inspector-General of Military Hospitals. It is a long quotation, but I could not curtail it; every word may be intelligently applied to our more recent controversy. It is, on the one hand, a melancholy picture of the mischief prejudice can do, and, on the other, a noble example of candour and manliness worthy of your imitation.

Before quitting the subject of army medical autho-

---

* William Fergusson, M.D., ' Notes and Recollections of a Professional Life.' 1846.

rities, I may remark, that considerable efforts were made to obtain for our soldiers the benefit of homœopathic treatment during the Crimean War in 1855, but they were frustrated by the medical autocracy; the same has occurred in India; the same, I suppose, everywhere; but, are such despotic restraints upon thought and the progress of medical science, at once so disgraceful to the ruler and degrading to the ruled, to be permitted to continue? It would have been a bright illumination of your posthumous character had you used your influence to dissipate, instead of to encourage, such evils, to break rather than to rivet the chain which for so many centuries has crippled research in medicine.

8. Before concluding your letter you again call us "pretenders;" let me therefore point out more clearly than I have yet done the leading mistake which has had firm possession of your mind from the first, and which has drawn you on until it has placed you in your present false position. The error appears very distinctly in your article in the 'Quarterly' in 1842, and it is the substratum of your letter in 'Fraser' in 1861. It is the error of your party, which looks upon homœopathy, either in ignorance or of set purpose, as if it were something which had sprung up *external* to the profession; as if it were like Mrs. Stephen's powder, St. John Long's ointment, or the "brandy and salt" cure, and required to be treated by medical men in the same manner. You wish the

qualified practitioner to keep himself aloof from it, to abstain carefully from any intercourse with those who advocate such an imposture, and thus to leave it to flourish and to die away, when the public are tired of it, as all other quackeries have died away before it. It will thus, you imagine, ere long, disappear, and, toge-ther with Perkinism and white mustard-seed, be laid in the tomb of all the Capulets.

" It cannot be otherwise than provoking," you say, " to those who have passed three or four years of the best part of their lives in endeavouring to make them-selves well acquainted with disease, in the wards of a hospital, to find that there are some among their patients who resort to them for advice only when their complaints have assumed a more painful or dangerous character; while they are set aside in ordinary cases which involve a smaller amount of anxiety and respon-sibility, in favour of some homœopathic doctor, who, very probably, never studied disease at all. But it cannot be helped. In all times there have been pre-tenders who have persuaded a certain part of the public that they have some peculiar knowledge of a royal road to cure, which those of the regular craft have not. It is homœopathy now; it was something else formerly; and, if homœopathy were to be extin-guished, there would be something else in its place. The medical profession must be contented to let the thing take its course."

Now, this would be excellent advice, if the fact were as you represent it; but your supposition is not true. Homœopathy is not, and never was, external to the profession; it originated *within* the profession, and still remains within it. It is a professional effort at improvement, and has no relationship whatever with such frauds as the metallic tractors of Perkins; if it had, all that would be required of the profession would be to furnish a Dr. Haygarth, who could plainly expose the imposition. No, Sir Benjamin, it is as much within the profession as Harvey's discovery of the circulation of the blood, or Laennec's invention of the stethoscope, and those who have adopted it have met with similar treatment from their professional brethren. Harvey was hooted at as a "circulator," and the physician who first used the stethoscope in this country was cried down as " the man with the penny trumpet," and now we are called "globulists." And so it seems, as you say, that it cannot be helped but that discoverers and inventors and benefactors of mankind must be ridiculed and abused. But upon whom has the real disgrace ultimately fallen in the case of Harvey, and in that of Laennec? I need not, therefore, hesitate to anticipate the future vindication of those who have laboured in the present reformation of medicine, and the removal of the dishonour now lying on their heads, to rest finally on those of others.

Homœopathists are qualified practitioners; they stand upon your own platform, and cannot be pushed off it. They have passed " three or four years," and some of them many more, in endeavouring to make themselves well acquainted with disease. They are every whit as legal and as professional as your-

self, and therefore the advice you have so frequently given is of no avail; it is not applicable to
the state of the case, and it cannot be followed.

In like manner the resolutions of medical societies
and the ordinances of medical colleges cannot stand
their ground any better. If not rescinded voluntarily
and with some acknowledgment of error, they will be
abrogated by lawful authority, or torn to pieces by
the force of circumstances. No violent efforts at expulsion or exclusion can extinguish the light which
has been kindled; it may, perhaps, be smothered for
a time, but only to break out again afterwards with a
brighter flame.

Let medical men listen to wiser counsels; a divided
house may be restored to unity and peace, and the
present unhappy heartburnings and jealousies may
be banished by the exhibition of a more Christian
spirit, and by the adoption of more appropriate
measures. Let wrath, and anger, and clamour, and
evil speaking, be put away, and let men learn to be
just and kind one to another; let the obnoxious
college by-laws be withdrawn; let a general invitation to medical men be issued, to give the new
method a fair practical examination; let it be tried,
under fitting circumstances, in public institutions,
and let proper reports of all these trials be published;
and, on the part of homœopathists, let all unessential
matters be relinquished, and let them abstain from
words of provocation or triumph.

9. And now, Sir Benjamin, I think I have

noticed all the points of your letter. I have done so without shrinking from any of them, and as fully as the very limited time allowed me has permitted. I have not been able to make any references but those with which memory supplied me, but I have written freely and confidently from what my own observation and experience have taught me. The opportunity has enabled me to present the law of the new method in a modified form, which, while it makes it more comprehensive, will, I hope, also make it less objectionable to you and those who think with you; I have, for the first time, suggested a law for the selection of the dose, and I have introduced a drug of great value into the materia medica.

The painful part has been that this had to be done in opposition to one whom I was formerly led to consider a friend, and for whom, for a large part of my life, I have entertained a most sincere regard. My classical friends will remember one who was placed in a similar position: " Δόξειε δ' ἂν ἴσως βέλτιον εἶναι καὶ δεῖν ἐπὶ σωτηρίᾳ," &c.—it is one's duty, when the safety of truth is involved, to sacrifice one's private feelings; for though both are dear to us, it is a sacred duty to prefer the claims of truth.*

Farewell, Sir Benjamin, farewell. If we never meet again until we stand together before the Great White Throne, may we then meet in charity and peace; but, that we may do so on that august occasion, we must not leave this present life otherwise than in charity and peace.

* Aristotle, 'Eth. Nic.'

APPENDIX.

THE following is the letter of Sir B. Brodie, which is addressed to "J. S. S., Esq.," and printed in 'Fraser's Magazine' for September, 1861.

DEAR SIR,—You desire me to give you my opinion of what is called homœopathy. I can do so without any great labour to myself, and without making any exorbitant demand on your patience, as the question really lies in very small compass, and what I have to say on it may be expressed in very few words.

The subject may be viewed under different aspects. We may inquire, first, whether homœopathy be, of itself, of any value, or of no value at all? secondly, in what manner does it affect general society? and thirdly, in what relation does it stand to the medical profession?

I must first request of you to observe that, whatever I may think at present, I had originally no prejudice either in favour of or against this new system; nor do I believe that the members of the medical profession generally were in the first instance influenced by any feelings of this kind. The fact is, that the fault of the profession for the most part lies in the opposite direction. They are too much inclined to adopt any new theory or any new mode of treatment that may have been proposed; the younger and more inexperienced among them especially erring in this respect, and too frequently indulging themselves in the trial of novelties, disregarding old and established remedies. For myself, I assure you that, whatever opinion I may now hold, it has not been hastily formed. I have made myself sufficiently acquainted with several works which profess to disclose the mysteries of homœopathy, especially that of Hahnemann, the founder of the homœopathic sect, and those of Dr. Curie and Mr. Sharpe. The result is, that, with all the pains that I have been able to take, I have been unable to form any very distinct notion of the system which they profess to teach. They all indeed begin with laying down, as the foundation of it, the rule that *similia similibus curantur;* or, in plain English, that one disease is to be driven out of the body by artificially creating another disease similar to it. But there the resemblance ends. Hahnemann treats the subject in one way, Dr. Curie in another, and Mr. Sharpe in another way still. General principles are asserted on the evidence of the most doubtful and scanty facts; and the reasoning on them for the most part is thoroughly puerile and illogical. I do not ask you to take all this for granted, but would rather refer you to the books themselves; being satisfied that any one, though he may not be versed in the science of medicine, who possesses good sense, and who has any knowledge of the caution with which all scientific investigations should be conducted, will arrive at the same conclusions as myself.

But, subordinate to the rule to which I have just referred, there is another, which, by some of the homœopathic writers, is held to be of great importance, and which is certainly the more remarkable one of the two. The doses of medicine administered by ordinary practitioners are represented to be very much too large. It is unsafe to have recourse to them, unless reduced to an almost infinitesimal point; not only to the millionth, but sometimes even to the billionth of a grain. Now observe what this means. Supposing one drop of liquid medicine to be equivalent to one grain, then, in order to obtain the millionth part of that dose, you must dissolve that drop in thirteen gallons of water, and administer only one drop of that solution; while in order to obtain the billionth of a grain, you must dissolve the aforesaid drop in 217,014 hogsheads of water. Of course, it is plain that this could not practically be accomplished, except by successive dilutions; and this would be a troublesome process. Whether it be at all probable that any one ever undertook to carry it out, I leave you to judge. At any rate, I conceive that there is no reasonable person who would not regard the exhibition of medicine in so diluted a form as being equivalent to no treatment at all.

But however this may be, I may be met by the assertion that there is undoubted evidence that a great number of persons recover from their complaints under homœopathic treatment, and I do not pretend in the least degree to deny it. In a discourse addressed by myself to the students of St. George's Hospital, in the year 1838, I find the following remarks :—"There is another inquiry which should be always made, before you determine on the adoption of a particular method of treatment; what will happen in this case, if no remedies whatever be employed, if the patient be left altogether to nature or to the efforts of his own constitution ?   *   *   *   *   *   *   * The animal system is not like a clock, or a steam-engine, which, being broken, you must send to the clockmaker or engineer to mend it ; and which cannot be repaired otherwise. The living machine, unlike the works of human invention, has the power of repairing itself ; it contains within itself its own engineer, who, for the most part, requires no more than some very slight assistance at our hands." This truth admits, indeed, of a very large application. If the arts of medicine and surgery had never been invented, by far the greater number of those who suffer from bodily illness would have recovered nevertheless. An experienced and judicious medical practitioner knows this very well; and considers it to be his duty, in the great majority of cases, not so much to interfere by any active treatment, as to take care that nothing should obstruct the natural process of recovery ; and, to watch lest, in the progress of the case, any new circumstance should arise which would make his active interference necessary. If any one were to engage in practice, giving his patients nothing but a little distilled water, and enjoining a careful diet, and a prudent mode of life otherwise, a certain number of his patients would perish from the want of further help; but more would recover; and homœopathic globules are, I doubt not, quite as good as distilled water.

But this does not account for all the success of homœopathy. In this country there is a large proportion of individuals who have plenty of money, combined with a great lack of employment; and it is astonishing to what an extent such persons contrive to imagine diseases for themselves. There is no animal machine so perfect that there may not at times be some creaking in it. Want of exercise, irregularity as to diet, a little worry of mind—these, and a thousand other causes, may occasion uneasy feelings, to which constant attention and thinking of them will give a reality which they would not have had otherwise; and such feelings will disappear as well under the use of globules as they would under any other mode of treatment, or under no treatment all.

What I have now mentioned will go far towards explaining the success of homœopathy. But other circumstances occur every now and then, from which, when they do occur, it profits to a still greater extent. *Humanum est errare.* From the operation of this universal law medical practitioners are not exempt, any

more than statesmen, divines, lawyers, engineers, or
any other profession. There are cases in which there
is a greater chance of too much than too little being
done for the patient; and if a patient under such circumstances becomes the subject of homœopathic treatment, this being no treatment at all, he actually derives
benefit from the change.

In a discourse to which I have already alluded,
I thought it my duty to offer the following caution
to my pupils :—" The first question which should
present itself to you in the management of a particular
case is this : is the disease one of which the patient
may recover, or is it not? There are indeed too many
cases in which the patient's condition is so manifestly
hopeless, that the fact cannot be overlooked. Let
me, however, caution you that you do not in any instance arrive too hastily at this conclusion. Our knowledge is not so absolute and certain as to prevent even
well-informed persons being occasionally mistaken on
this point. This is true, especially with respect to the
affections of internal organs. Individuals have been
restored to health who were supposed to be dying of
disease in the lungs or mesenteric glands." * * *
" It is a good rule in the practice of our art, as in the
common affairs of life, for us to look on the favorable side of the question, as far as we can consistently
with reason do so." I might have added that hysteri-
cal affections are especially a source of error to not
very experienced practitioners, by simulating more
serious disease; seeming to resist for a time all the

efforts of art, and then all at once subsiding under any kind of treatment, or, just as well, under none at all. Now, if it should so happen that a medical practitioner, from want of knowledge, or from a natural defect of judgment, makes a mistake in his diagnosis, and the patient whom he had unsuccessfully treated afterwards recovers under the care of another practitioner, it is simply said " Dr. A. was mistaken ;" and it is not considered as any thing very remarkable that the symptoms should subside while under the care of Dr. B. But if, on the other hand, the recovery takes place under the care of a homœopathist, or any other empiric, the circumstance excites a much larger portion of attention ; and we really cannot very well wonder that, with such knowledge as they possess of these matters, the empiric should gain much credit with the public.

So far the practical result would seem to be that homœopathy can be productive of no great harm ; and indeed, considering it to be no treatment at all, whenever it is a substitute for bad treatment, it must be the better of the two. But there is great harm nevertheless. There are numerous cases in which spontaneous recovery is out of the question ; in which sometimes the life or death of the patient, and at other times the comfort or discomfort of his existence for a long time to come, depends on the prompt application of active and judicious treatment. In such cases homœopathy is neither more nor less than a mischievous absurdity ; and I do not hesitate to say that a very

large number of persons have fallen victims to the
faith which they reposed in it, and to the consequent
delay in having recourse to the use of proper remedies.
It is true that it very rarely happens, when any symptoms show themselves which give real alarm to the
patient or his friends, that they do not dismiss the
homœopathist and send for a regular practitioner;
but it may well be that by this time the mischief is
done, the case being advanced beyond the reach of
art.

That the habit of resorting to homœopathic treatment which has prevailed in some parts of society
should have occasioned much dissatisfaction among
the mass of medical practitioners, is no matter of wonder.   It cannot be otherwise than provoking, to those
who have passed three or four years of the best part
of their lives in endeavouring to make themselves well
acquainted with disease, in the wards of a hospital, to
find that there are some among their patients who resort to them for advice only when their complaints
have assumed a more painful or dangerous character;
while they are set aside in ordinary cases, which involve a smaller amount of anxiety and responsibility,
in favour of some homœopathic doctor, who, very
probably, never studied disease at all.   But it cannot
be helped.   In all times there have been pretenders,
who have persuaded a certain part of the public that
they have some peculiar knowledge of a royal road to
cure, which those of the regular craft have not.   It is
homœopathy now; it was something else formerly;

and if homœopathy were to be extinguished, there would be something else in its place. The medical profession must be contented to let the thing take its course; and they will best consult their own dignity, and the good of the public, by saying as little as possible about it. The discussions as to the evils of homœopathy which have sometimes taken place at public meetings, have quite an opposite effect to that which they were intended to produce. They have led some to believe that homœopathists are rather a persecuted race, and have given to the system which they pursue an importance which it would never have had otherwise; just as any absurd or fanatical sect in religion would gain proselytes if it could only make others believe that it was an object of jealousy and persecution. After all, the harm done to the regular profession is not so great as many suppose it to be; a very large proportion of the complaints about which homœopathists are consulted being really no complaints at all, for which a respectable practitioner would scarcely think it right to prescribe.

There was a time when many of the medical profession held the opinion that not only homœopathy, but all other kinds of quackery, ought to be put down by the strong hand of the law. I imagine that there are very few who hold that opinion now. The fact is, that the thing is impossible; and even if it were possible—as it is plain that the profession cannot do all that is wanted of them, by curing all kinds of disease, and making men immortal—such an interference with the liberty of individuals to consult whom they please would be absurd and wrong. As it now is, the law forbids the employment in any public institution of any one who is not registered as being a qualified medical practitioner, after a due examination by some of the constituted authorities ; and it can go no further. The only effectual opposition which the medical profession can offer to homœopathy, is by individually taking all possible pains to avoid, on their own part, those errors of diagnosis by means of which, more than anything else, the professors of homœopathy thrive and flourish ; by continuing in all ways to act honorably by the public ; at the same time never being induced, either by good nature or by any motives of self-interest, to appear to give their sanction to a system which they know to have no foundation in reality. To join with homœopathists in attendance on cases of either medical or surgical disease, would be neither wise nor honest. The object of a medical consultation is the good of the patient; and we cannot suppose that any such result can arise from the interchange of opinions, where the views entertained, or professed to be entertained, by one of the parties as to the nature and treatment of disease, are wholly unintelligible to the other.

I am, dear Sir,

Yours, &c.,

B. C. BRODIE.

The following letter from Sir B. Brodie, on the

same subject, has been published in the medical journals, dated Betchworth, July 27th, 1861.

"I feel confident that our profession generally will do me the justice to believe that I would not, either directly or indirectly, do anything that would in any way sanction a system so absurd and nonsensical as I know the so-called homœopathy to be.

"Having been in the habit of seeing, especially at my own house, many patients attended by practitioners of whom I had no knowledge, I cannot say that I may not by accident have occasionally seen some one attended by a homœopathist; but I have never knowingly done so; and I do not think that any well-educated medical practitioner can honestly meet one of these homœopathists in consultation. The only object of a consultation is to do good to the patient; and it is out of the question to suppose that any interchange of idea with one in whose professed opinions we have not the smallest faith, and whose notions, indeed, we cannot comprehend, can tend to this result."

––––––––––

I have alluded to Mr. Fergusson, one of Her Majesty's surgeons-extraordinary, in consequence of the manner in which he has acted in the matter of consultations with medical men who have adopted homœopathic practice; it seems necessary, therefore, to add his letters to those of Sir B. Brodie. The

whole will, no doubt, be looked upon hereafter as
an edifying but melancholy picture of the condition
of the medical profession in England in the year
1861.

I.

The 'Lancet,' May 8th, 1858.

" To the Editor of the ' Lancet.'

" SIR,—In compliance with your courteous notice
in the 'Lancet' last week, I beg to state that I accompanied Dr. Bell to Lincolnshire, on the 26th of February last, to see an urgent surgical case.   I have not
seen the patient since.

" I do not consult with homœopaths ; and I am not
and never have been, in attendance on a noble duke
in conjunction with a homœopath.

" I have no faith in homœopathy.   I give no encouragement to homœopaths to consult me.   I never
refuse my surgical assistance when it is called for in
any urgent or important case ; and *were a fatal result
to arise from any neglect of mine, I should consider my
conduct unjustifiable.*

" I have the honour to be, Sir,

" Your obedient, humble servant,

(Signed)   " WM. FERGUSSON.

" George St., Hanover Square ;

" May 7th, 1858."

II.

The 'Lancet,' July 20th, 1861.

" The late Elections at the Royal College of Surgeons.

" *To the Editor of the ' Lancet.'*

" SIR,—Three years ago a clamour was raised against me for alleged communion with homœopaths. In consequence of an urgent and courteous appeal on your part, I sent a note of explanation, which you did me the favour to publish in your number for May 8th, 1858. That explanation was accepted by some, but not by others; although, as far as I know, my name has not since been publicly associated with the subject until within the last few weeks.

" Recent events at the College of Surgeons have given occasion to a revival of the clamour referred to, and my orthodoxy has been again challenged. I might refer to the note above alluded to, as my answer now, as it was then; but years make a difference in various ways, and I shall, with your leave, say a little more than when I last addressed you.

" The fault of which I was accused three years ago, was that I travelled in company with a homœopath to relieve a gentleman of retention of urine, when the regular surgeon in attendance had failed; and I was further accused of holding consultations with homœopaths. The former charge I admitted, and the latter I distinctly denied. In addition, I stated that ' I had no faith in homœopathy,' and that ' I gave no en-

couragement to homœopaths to consult me.' I added
further, that I never refused my surgical services in
any important case where they might be required, and
*would hold my conduct unjustifiable if any evil or
fatal result ensued from negligence or refusal .on my
part.*

"To all these views I hold as strongly now as I did
at the time in question. I still do not consult with
homœopaths; I still have no faith in homœopathy,
and I still give no encouragement to homœopaths to
consult me.

"I never intended, and do not wish now, to have
or leave room for any quibble on these points. I
have been told that to meet a homœopath, in any way
in a case, is to consult with him, and that therefore
my denial is worthless; that such meeting amounts to
a consultation. With those who take this view I at
once plead guilty. I am occasionally consulted by
homœopaths, (as I know other surgeons are,) and,
hearing their history of a case in clearer terms than
from the patient or a friend, I give a surgical opinion;
with this the interview ends. From first to last there
is not a word about homœopathy introduced; but
should there be, I invariably let the patient know that
I have no faith in such doctrine, and that I am giving
my opinion solely as a surgeon.

"I am not aware that I have met with any man
who has stronger views, prepossessions, or objections
against homœopathy, than I have. No homœopath
can say that I ever ceded to him one tittle on homœo-

pathic principles; and as a public teacher of thirty-five years' standing, I appeal to my numerous pupils with the utmost confidence that they will free me from the imputation of ever having encouraged such doctrines.

" I have the honour to be, Sir,

" Your most obedient servant,

(Signed) " WILLIAM FERGUSSON, F.R.C.S.

" George Street, Hanover Square; July, 1861."

III.

The ' Medical Circular,' August 21st, 1861.

" *To the Editor of the ' Medical Circular.'*

" SIR,—The explanations I offered in my lettter to the ' Lancet ' of the 20th July last, regarding my alleged communion with homœopaths, not appearing satisfactory to the profession, I beg to state that *for the future I shall feel it incumbent on me to decline any meeting or so-called consultation with homœopathic practitioners.*

" Enjoying a large share of professional confidence, and holding various important public appointments, I should consider myself unworthy of such honours were I, *at the present time*, to offer any objections to the expressed wishes and declared opinions of my professional brethren.

"I am, &c.,

(Signed) "WM. FERGUSSON.

" 16, George Street, Hanover Square;

"August 12th, 1861."

Alas! for conscience, poor brow-beaten conscience, when, after all the vindications it can offer, only a tumult is made, and the "clamour" increases!

And so Mr. Fergusson's conscience has been telling him, for three years past, that *to refuse to help a surgical* patient, at the request of any professional brother, would be *unjustifiable conduct*.

But the medical brother holds views on *medical* treatment which Mr. Fergusson has not investigated, and therefore does not understand; a "clamour" is raised, his conscience must yield and be silenced, and the patient be refused his help, though a fatal result ensue!

"Happy is he that *condemneth not himself* in that thing which he alloweth."

LIST

OF

HOMŒOPATHIC WORKS

PUBLISHED AND IMPORTED BY

HENRY TURNER & CO.,

HOMŒOPATHIC CHEMISTS AND MEDICAL PUBLISHERS,

77, FLEET STREET, LONDON, E.C.;

41, PICCADILLY, & 15, MARKET STREET, MANCHESTER.

** All Books, the published price of which is 1s. or upwards, are delivered post free to any address within the limits of the reduced Book Postage.

ACKWORTH (Dr. E.) MY CONVERSION TO HOMŒOPATHY. Third Edition. Sewed, 2d.

AMERICAN HOMŒOPATHIC REVIEW.

*** According to an announcement in the last number issued, this serial will not be discontinued, as expected, but will in future be conducted under the immediate supervision of Drs. B. F. Joslin, P. P. Wells, Carroll Dunham, and H. M. Smith. Each issue is supplied immediately on its arrival in this country. Terms, 14s. per annum post free, payable in advance. Single copies, 1s. 2d.

ARNICA, CALENDULA, CANTHARIDES, CAUSTICUM, RHUS, AND Urtica as External Remedies; comprising plain Directions for the Use of these Medicines in Cases of Accident, Operation, Gout, Rheumatism, &c. Sewed, 1s.

ASIATIC CHOLERA; DIRECTIONS FOR THE DOMESTIC USE OF Homœopathic Medicine in. 6d. per dozen, or 3s. 6d. per 100.

BAYES (Dr. WM.) ADDRESS TO THE GOVERNORS OF ADDENbrooke's Hospital. Sewed 6d.

BAYES (Dr. WM.) TWO SIDES TO A QUESTION: A FEW OBSERvations on Mr. Braithwaite's ' Temperate Examination of Homœopathy.' Second Edition, with Emendations and Additions. Sewed, 6d.

BECKER (Dr. A. C.) CONSUMPTION, DISEASES OF THE EYE, Constipation and Dentition, in 1 vol. Cloth, 5s.

BECKER (Dr. A.C.) ALLOPATHY, HAHNEMANNISM, AND RATIONAL Homœopathy. Sewed, 1s.

BELLUOMINI (Dr. J.) SCARLATINA AND ITS TREATMENT HOmœopathically. Sewed, 1s.

BŒNNINGHAUSEN (Dr. C. VON.) ESSAY ON THE HOMŒOPA-
thic Treatment of Intermittent Fevers. Translated and edited by Dr. C.
J. HEMPEL. Cloth, 2s. 6d.

BŒNNINGHAUSEN (Dr. C. VON.) THERAPEUTIC POCKET-BOOK
for the Use of Homœopathic Physicians. Edited by Dr. C. J. HEMPEL.
Cloth, 10s.

BŒNNINGHAUSEN (Dr. C. VON.) SIDES OF THE BODY AND
Drug Affinities—Homœopathic Exercises. Translated and Edited by Dr.
C. J. HEMPEL. In stiff cover, 1s. 6d.

BRITISH JOURNAL OF HOMŒOPATHY. Edited by Drs. DRYSDALE,
DUDGEON, and ATKIN. Published Quarterly. Price to Subscribers
18s. per annum, post free; single copies, 5s.
    ₊ This is the *oldest-established Medical Quarterly* in Great Britain.

BRITISH WORKMAN'S GUIDE TO HOMŒOPATHIC TREATMENT:
compiled chiefly from the Works of Drs. GUERNSEY, MALAN, HERING,
and MOORE, with the object of rendering the domestic practice of Homœopathy in common ailments as simple as possible, to meet the requirements
of the working-classes. Limp cloth, 1s.

BRYANT (Dr. J.) RIVAL SCHOOLS OF MEDICINE; OR, HOMŒO-
pathy verses Allopathy. Sewed, 1s.

BRYANT (Dr. J.) POCKET MANUAL; OR, REPERTORY OF HO-
mœopathy Alphabetically and Nosologically Arranged. Second Edition.
Bound, 6s.

CASPARI'S HOMŒOPATHIC DOMESTIC PHYSICIAN. Edited by F.
HARTMANN, M.D., Author of "Acute and Chronic Diseases." Transla-
ted from the Eighth German Edition, and enriched by a Treatise on
Anatomy and Physiology. Embellished with 30 Illustrations, by Dr.
W. P. Esrey. Bound, 8s.

CHANNING (Dr. W.) THE REFORMATION OF MEDICAL
Science, demanded by Inductive Philosophy. A Discourse delivered before
the New-York Physician's Society. Second Edition. Sewed, 1s. 6d.

CHEPMELL (Dr. E. C.) DOMESTIC HOMŒOPATHY RESRICTED
to its legitimate sphere of practice; together with rules for diet and
regimen. Eighth Edition, revised and improved. Cloth, 6s.

CHEPMELL (Dr. E. C.) PRACTICAL GUIDE TO DOMESTIC
Homœopathy, with a selection of fourteen Remedies. Limp cloth, 1s.

CHOLERA AND ITS HOMŒOPATHIC TREATMENT. With Sta-
tistics showing the successful treatment of this epidemic with Homœopathic Remedies, giving sanitary precautions and elementary instructions
for its treatment. First series. 1d., or 7s. per 100.

COCKBURN (Dr. SAMUEL). THE TWO SYSTEMS OF MEDICINE
Cure Explained and Contrasted. Limp cloth, 2s.
    " We recommend this little book as one of the most readable and reliable
exposés of the Allopathic and Homœopathic Systems we have met with."—
British Journal of Homœopathy.
    " The whole of the book is well and pleasantly written."—*Monthly Homœo-
pathic Review.*

COCKBURN (Dr. SAMUEL). EXPOSITION OF THE HOMŒO-pathic Law, with a Refutation of some of the chief Objections advanced against Homœopathy: a Lecture delivered in Glasgow under the auspices of the Glasgow Homœopathic Association. Sewed, 3d.

COE (Dr. GLOVER). CONCENTRATED ORGANIC MEDICINES, their Therapeutic Properties and Clinical Employments. Second Edition. Cloth, 10s. 6d.

CRAIG (Dr. W. S.) HOMŒOPATHY: A LETTER IN ANSWER TO Mr. Braithwaite's 'Temperate Examination of Homœopathy.' Sewed, 2d.

CROSERIO (Dr. C.) HOMŒOPATHIC MANUAL OF OBSTETRICS; or, A Treatise on the Aid the Art of Midwifery may derive from Homœo-pathy. Cloth, 4s.

CURTIS AND LILLIE (Drs.) EPITOME OF HOMŒOPATHIC Practice. Compiled chiefly from Jahr. Rückert, Beauvais, Bœnninghausen, &c. Second Enlarged Edition. Cloth, 4s.

DENHAM (Dr. W. H.) THE FOLLY AND MISCHIEF OF USING Purgative Medicines. Sewed, 2d.

DOMESTIC HOMŒOPATHY SIMPLIFIED; OR, TWELVE REME-dies and their Use in Common Ailments. Sewed, 6d.

DOUGLAS (Dr. J. S.) THE HOMŒOPATHIC TREATMENT OF IN-termittent Fevers. 2s.

DRUMMOND (Dr. J.) HOMŒOPATHY AMONGST THE ALLOPATHS, being a collection of evidence favorable to the tenets of Hahnemann and his followers, EXTRACTED FROM THE STANDARD WORKS OF THE OLD SCHOOL. In stiff cover, 1s.

DRURY (Dr. W. V.) FATTY DISEASE OF THE HEART AND SOFT-ening, with Homœopathic Treatment. Sewed 1s.

DRURY (Dr. W. V.) HOMŒOPATHIC GUIDE FOR THE TREAT-ment of Accidents. Cloth, 2s. 6d.

DRYSDALE AND RUSSELL'S INTRODUCTION TO THE STUDY OF Homœopathy. Cloth, 4s. 6d.

DRYSDALE, DUDGEON, AND BLACK (Drs.) THE HAHNEMANN Materia Medica Pura, Part I. In stiff cover, 7s.

DUDGEON (Dr. R. E.) LECTURES ON THE THEORY AND PRAC-tice of Homœopathy. Cloth, 7s. 6d.

> "A complete epitome of the history and development of Homœopathy."
> —*Civil Service Gazette.*
> "The volume teems with interesting matter."—*British Banner.*

" We cordially recommend it as suitable for a place in every Homœopathic physician's library."—*Philadelphia Journal of Homœopathy.*

" We commend Dr. Dudgeon's work to the public and the faculty."— *Globe.*

" A more useful exposition of our system was never read."—*The Homœopathist.*

" We have never seen so full and comprehensive an account of the principles and practice of Homœopathy."—*Nonconformist.*

" The best acquisition to Homœopathic literature during the whole year, and a better work than any other treating on the same subject."—*Dr. C. Hering.*

ESREY (DR. W. P.) TREATISE ON ANATOMY AND PHYSIOLOGY. With 30 Illustrations.   Cloth, 2s. 6d.

ESREY (DR. W. P.) MATERIA MEDICA OF AMERICAN PROVINGS. With Repertory.   Cloth, 6s.

FLETCHER'S (DR. JOHN G.) ELEMENTS OF GENERAL PATHOLOGY. Edited by DRS. DRYSDALE and RUSSELL.   Cloth, 10s. 6d.

GLIMPSES OF HAHNEMANN, THE FOUNDER OF HOMŒOPATHY: A compilation from various sources, illustrative of the Life and Character of Hahnemann.   Extra bound, gilt edges, 2s.

GOLLMANN (Dr. W.)   THE HOMŒOPATHIC GUIDE IN ALL DIS-eases of the Urinary and Sexual Organs.   Translated, with Additions, by DR. C. J. HEMPEL. Cloth, 7s. 6d.

GUERNSEY'S DOMESTIC PRACTICE.   Abridged, Revised, and Edited by Dr. THOMAS.   Containing a plain description of Diseases, and in-structions for their Cure, giving express directions in each case for the administration of the Remedy, both in Tinctures and Globules; contain-ing also chapters on Varieties of Constitution and Temperament, the Pulse, the Urine, General Diagnosis, Diet, Hygiene, Climate, and Bathing, and a Materia Medica and Glossary.   Cloth, 5s.

⁎ This edition of Guernsey's ' Domestic Practice ' is divested of every-thing which is objectionable in a book of general reference for the use of families.

" Of all Domestic Treatises we give the preference to Dr. Guernsey's."— *North American Journal of Homœopathy.*

" Dr. Guernsey's Book of ' Domestic Practice' is a reliable and useful work. It is especially adapted to the service of well-educated heads of families."— *John F. Gray, M.D.*

GUERNSEY (DR. E.) THE GENTLEMAN'S HAND-BOOK OF HO-mœopathy; especially for Travellers, and for Domestic Practice.   Second Edition.   Cloth, 4s.

HAHNEMANN (DR. S.) MATERIA MEDICA PURA.   Translated by DR. C. J. HEMPEL, in 1 vol.   Half bound, 30s.

HAHNEMANN (DR. S.) CHRONIC DISEASES: THEIR SPECIFIC Nature and Homœopathic Treatment.   Translated and Edited by DR. C. J. HEMPEL, with a Preface by DR. C. HERING.   5 vols., cloth, 35s.

HAHNEMANN (Dr. S.) ORGANON OF HOMŒOPATHIC MEDICINE Fourth American Edition, with Improvements and Additions from the last German Edition, together with Dr. Hering's Introductory Remarks. Cloth, 6s.

HAHNEMANN, PORTRAIT OF. Engraved on Steel. By Woodman, from a Painting by G. F. Hering, Esq.
This superb engraving was taken from a portrait in the possession of William Leaf, Esq., and is considered by those best qualified to judge, the best extant of the venerable founder of Homœopathy.
Prints, 10s. 6d.; Proofs, on India paper (only very few remain), 21s.

HAHNEMANN, STATUETTE OF, IN PARIAN. By Mr. KIRK, A.R.H.A. (only very few remain), 63s.
The most perfect and truthful statuette or bust ever produced.

HARPER (Dr. J. P.) HOMŒOPATHY TESTED BY FACTS: being a collection of cases illustrative of the Homœopathic action of remedial agents. Third Edition, sewed, 6d.

HARTLAUB AND WOOD (Drs.) THE CHILD'S HOMŒOPATHIC Physician; or, Full and Plain Advice to Parents on the Management of Infants and Children, and on the Treatment of their Disorders. Translated from Dr. Hartlaub's Fourth Foreign Edition, with the addition of Cases illustrating the Treatment, and many New Chapters. By Dr. NEVILLE WOOD, Cloth, 5s.

This book describes the symptoms, causes, and probable termination of every disorder, and gives plain and precise instructions as to the general and medicinal treatment of the case.
" We very cordially recommend this book. * * * a very valuable addition to the *best* class of domestic books."—*Monthly Homœopathic Review.*
" Dr. Neville Wood has done well in presenting this work to the public."—*Notes of a New Truth.*
" The cases are well selected."—*British Journal of Homœopathy.*
" The present treatise will be found admirably useful."—*Daily Telegraph.*
" Of all domestic guides, it is certainly the most intelligible. Homœopathic mothers will find it invaluable. * * * As a guide to the believer, this work is indispensable."—*Constitutional Press.*

HARTMAN (Dr. F.) CHRONIC DISEASES AND THEIR HOMŒO-pathic Treatment. Translated and Revised from the Third German Edition, with additions. By Dr. C. J. HEMPEL. 2 vols., cloth, 15s.

HARTMAN (Dr. F.) DISEASES OF CHILDREN, AND THEIR Homœopathic Treatment. Translated, with Remarks. By Dr. C. J. HEMPEL. Cloth, 10s.

HARTMAN (Dr. F.) PRACTICAL OBSERVATIONS ON SOME OF the chief Homœopathic Remedies. Translated from the German. By Dr. OKIE. Cloth, 5s.

HASTINGS (Dr. HUGH) CONSUMPTION, ITS PREVENTION AND Cure (Homœopathically). Sewed, 6d.

HASTINGS (Dr. HUGH) A DIALOGUE ON THE THEORY AND Practice of Homœopathy and Allopathy. Third Edition, sewed, 6d.

HASTINGS (Dr. HUGH) SCARLATINA AND DIPHTHERIA, THEIR Treatment and Prevention. Second edition. Sewed 6d.

HAYWARD (DR. J. W.) ALLOPATHY AND HOMŒOPATHY CON-
trasted.
Part 1, Medicine—its origin and early history; Allopathy—what it is; Ho-
mœopathy—what it is? Sewed, 3d.
Part 2, the origin and early history of Allopathy and Homœopathy.
Sewed, 2d.

HEMPEL (DR. C. J.) A TREATISE ON THE USE OF ARNICA IN
cases of Contusions, Wounds, Sprains, Lacerations of the Solids, Con-
cussions, Paralyses, Rheumatisms, Soreness of the Nipples, &c. &c., with
a number of Cases illustrative of the use of that Drug. Sewed, 1s.

HEMPEL (DR. C. J.) COMPLETE REPERTORY OF THE HOMŒO-
pathic Materia Medica. 1224 pp. Bound, 30s.

> " We have now before us the result of Dr. Hempel's incessant labours, in
> the shape of a portly volume of upwards of 1200 pages, for which he deserves
> the best thanks of the Homœopathic body at large. This volume will be a
> great acquisition to all the practitioners of our art, as it will facilitate very
> much their search for the appropriate remedy. We have already made ex-
> tensive use of it. Thanking Dr. Hempel most heartily for his " Repertory,"
> we commend it confidently to our English colleagues. It will be found use-
> ful by all; and it will, in many cases, guide the practitioner to the ready dis-
> covery of an appropriate remedy when all the other works hitherto published
> in our language would leave him in the lurch."—*British Journal of Ho-
> mœopathy.*

HEMPEL (DR. C. J.) ECLECTICISM IN MEDICINE; OR, A
Critical Review of the leading Medical Doctrines. An Inaugural Thesis
presented at the New York University, in March, 1845. By Dr. C. J.
HEMPEL. Sewed, 1s. 6d.

HEMPEL (DR. C. J.) ORGANON OF SPECIFIC HOMŒOPATHY;
or, an Inductive Exposition of the Principles of the Homœopathic
Healing Art, addressed to Physicians and Intelligent Laymen. Cloth, 5s.

HEMPEL (DR. C. J.) HOMŒOPATHY, A PRINCIPLE IN NATURE,
its Scientific Universality unfolded, its Development and Philosophy
explained, and its applicability to the Treatment of Diseases shown.
Cloth, 6s.

HEMPEL (DR. C. J.) A NEW AND COMPREHENSIVE SYSTEM OF
Materia Medica and Therapeutics. Arranged upon a Physiologico-Patho-
logical Basis, for the use of Practitioners and Students of Medicine.
1220 pp. Bound in calf, 25s.

> " In this work, the subject of Homœopathic Materia Medica and Thera-
> peutics is presented, as it should be, in connection with Pathology and Phy-
> siology. It is the concurrent testimony of those who have seen the work
> that, in this splendid volume, Homœopathic Materia Medica is, for the first
> time in the history of Homœopathy, presented as a scientific system of Thera-
> peutics. Homœopathic physicians will find this work a reliable and most
> comprehensive guide in the treatment of disease. Students and Allopathic
> practitioners may acquire a thorough and comparatively easy knowledge of
> Homœopathy by a perusal of its pages; we would even venture to assert that
> Homœopathic physicians of experience may read this work with profit and
> pleasure. In no work that we know of is the subject of Homœopathy pre-
> sented to the inquiring mind in the same broad and comprehensive sense as
> in the present volume. We feel justified in recommending it to the profes-
> sion as a standard work, which every friend of Homœopathy should possess."

HEMPEL AND BEAKLEY (Drs.) MANUAL OF HOMŒOPATHIC
Theory and Practice. An Elementary Treatise on the Homœopathic
Treatment of Surgical Diseases. Cloth, 12s.

HELMUTH (Dr. W. T.) SURGERY, AND ITS ADAPTATION TO
Homœpathic Practice. Illustrated with numerous Wood Engravings.
Bound in sheep, 15s.

HERING (Dr. C.) HOMŒOPATHIC DOMESTIC PHYSICIAN. The
only authorised English edition recognised by the Author, thoroughly
revised and reformed from the original, and augmented by numerous
additions. Cloth, 8s.

HIRSCHEL'S RULES AND EXAMPLES FOR THE STUDY OF
Pharmacodynamics. Translated by THOMAS HAYLE. Cloth, 5s.

HITCHMAN (Dr. WM.) CONSUMPTION, ITS NATURE, PREVEN-
tion, and Homœopathic Treatment, with illustrations of Homœopathic
practice. Cloth, 3s.

> "This Treatise is the most complete work on the subject of Consumption
> that has ever been issued by the Homœopathic press. It shows most conclu-
> sively that Consumption may be cured by Homœopathic remedies if the
> treatment is not delayed too long. The nature and course of this serious dis-
> order are very lucidly explained in this interesting work, and the Homœopa-
> thic treatment is illustrated by a number of interesting cases. No physician,
> after studying this volume, can be at a loss how to treat Consumption succes-
> fully, if the case is not absolutely beyond the reach of treatment. The
> volume is neatly got up, and should meet, as it undoubtedly will, with a ready
> sale."

> "Hitchman on 'Consumption' is the best monogram in Homœopathic
> literature—of great practical interest, scholarly, and beautifully written."—
> North American Journal of Homœopathy.

HILL AND HUNT'S HOMŒOPATHIC PRACTICE OF SURGERY,
together with Operative Surgery. Illustrated by 240 Engravings. Bound
in sheep, 17s.

HOLLAND (Dr. G. C.) ORIGIN AND NATURE OF DISEASE,
and the Physiological Action of Auxiliary Remedies in connection with
Homœopathic Treatment. Cloth, 9s.

HOLCOMB (Dr. W. H.) THE SCIENTIFIC BASIS OF HOMŒOPATHY.
Cloth, 5s. 6d.

HOLCOMB (Dr. W. H.) YELLOW FEVER, AND ITS HOMŒOPATHIC
Treatment. Cloth, 2s.

HOMŒOPATHIC PHARMACOPŒIA AND POSOLOGY. Compiled from
the Works of Buchner and Gruner, also the French Works of Jahr, with
Original Contributions. By Dr. C. J. HEMPEL. Cloth, 8s.

HORNER (Dr. F. R.) REASONS FOR ADOPTING THE RATIONAL System of Medicine, being a Letter to the Governors of the Hull General Infirmary. Fifth Edition. (Twenty Thousand.) Sewed, 6d.

> " Here is a man, occupying a most distinguished position as an allopathic physician, who, after investigating principles, brings them to the test of practice, and then, being convinced of their truth, at once heartily adopts them."
> —*Manchester Weekly Advertiser.*

HORNER (Dr. JONAH) ON HEALTH; what Preserves, what Destroys, and what Restores it. Limp cloth, 1s. 6d.

HOUSEHOLD HOMŒOPATHIST; or, MOTHER'S GUIDE TO PRACTICE. Cloth, 1s. 6d.

HUGHES (Rd., M.R.C.S.) ON THE PRESENT STATE OF THE Physiology and Pathology of the Nervous System. Sewed, 1s.

HUFELAND. EUCHIRIDION MEDICUM; or, THE PRACTICE OF Medicine. The result of Fifty years' experience of the Physician in Ordinary to the late King of Prussia, and Professor in the University of Berlin. Second American Edition. Translated from the Sixth German Edition by Dr. BRUCHHAUSEN. Cloth, 12s. 6d.

HUMPHREYS (Prof. Dr. F.) CHOLERA AND ITS HOMŒOPATHIC Treatment. Cloth, 2s.

HUMPHREY'S (Dr.) DYSENTERY, AND ITS HOMŒOPATHIC Treatment. Containing also a Repertory and numerous Cases. Cloth, 2s. 6d.

JAHR'S NEW MANUAL OF HOMŒOPATHIC PRACTICE. Edited, with Annotations by Dr. A. GERALD HULL from Jahr's last Paris Edition. Fourth American Edition being a New Edition of the Symptomatology. Edited with Annotations by Dr. F. G. SNELLING. In Two vols. Half bound, 30s.

JAHR (Dr. G. H. G.) CLINICAL GUIDE; or, POCKET-REPERTORY for the Treatment of Acute and Chronic Diseases. Translated from the German by C. J. HEMPEL, M.D. Bound, 7s. 6d.

JAHR (Dr. G. H. G.) DISEASES OF THE SKIN; or, ALPHABETICAL Repertory of the Skin-Symptoms and External Alterations of Substance; together with the Morbid Phenomena observed in the Glandular, Osseous, Mucous, and Circulatory Symptoms, arranged with Pathological Remarks on the Diseases of the Skin. Edited by C. J. HEMPEL, M.D. Bound, 5s.

JAHR'S NEW MANUAL OF THE HOMŒOPATHIC MATERIA Medica, with Possart's Additions. Arranged with reference to well-authenticated Observations at the Sick-bed, and accompanied by an Alphabetical Repertory, to facilitate and secure the selection of a suitable remedy in any given case. Fifth Edition, revised and enlarged by the Author. SYMPTOMATOLOGY and REPERTORY. Translated and Edited by C. J. HEMPEL, M.D. Bound, 17s. 6d.

JAHR (DR. G. H. G.) THE HOMŒOPATHIC TREATMENT OF Diseases of Females and Infants at the Breast. Translated from the French by C. J. HEMPEL, M.D. Bound, 10s. 6d.

JAHR ON MENTAL DISEASES. Translated by Dr. GALLOWAY. Cloth, 10s.

JAHR'S NEW MANUAL OR SYMPTOMEN CODEX. Translated, with important and extensive additions from various sources, by Dr. C. J. HEMPEL, assisted by Dr. QUIN; with revisions and notes by Dr. J. F. GRAY. Contributions by Drs. A. GERALD HULL and G. W. COOKE, of New York, and Drs. C. HERING, J. JEANES, C. NEIDHARD, W. WILLIAMSON, and J. KITCHEN, with a preface by Dr. HERING. In 3 vols. Bound, £6 6s. (Scarce.)

JONES (DR. ELIJAH U.) DRY COUGH OR TUSSIS-SICCA. Sewed, 6d.

JOSLIN (DR. B. F.) PRINCIPLES OF HOMŒOPATHY. In a Series of Lectures. Cloth, 2s.

JOSLIN (DR. B. F.) HOMŒOPATHIC TREATMENT OF CHOLERA, including Repertories for this Disease and for Summer Complaints. Third Edition, with Additions. Cloth, 2s. 6d.

JOSLIN (DR. B. F.) THE LAW OF CURE. Address before the American Institute of Homœopathy, held at Philadelphia, June 13th. Sewed, 1s.

KREUSSLER (DR. E.) THE HOMŒOPATHIC TREATMENT OF Acute and Chronic Diseases. Translated from the German, with important Additions and Revisions, by CHARLES J. HEMPEL. Small print, to make it convenient for the pocket. Cloth, 5s.

MACLIMONT (DR. R.) HOMŒOPATHY THE ONLY LAW OF CURE, being a simple and concise Exposition of the System, with an Appendix containing the record of a few cases from the Note Book of the writer. Post 8vo, sewed, 3d.

MACLIMONT (DR. R.) THE IMPORTANCE OF CHANGE OF CLIMATE in the First Stage of Pulmonary Consumption, embracing the result of some years' experience of the Climates of Madeira, Rome, Nice, Mentone, etc., in Affections of the Chest. Sewed, 1s.

M'MANUS (DR. F. R.) AN ADDRESS DELIVERED AT THE SEVENteenth Annual Meeting of the American Institute of Homœopathy, in June, 1860. Sewed, 1s.

MALAN (DR. H. V.) POCKET-BOOK OF HOMŒOPATHY. Containing concise Directions for the Treatment of some of the most common Ailments in Families. Fourth Edition, revised. Limp cloth, 2s.

MALAN (DR. H. V.) ANSWER TO THE QUESTION. "HOW CAN such small Doses have any Effect?" Third Edition. Sewed, 3d.

MALAN (DR. H. V.) WHAT TO DO IN CASE OF CHOLERA. 7s. per hundred.

MARSTON (Dr. C. H.) HOMŒOPATHY AND SIR BENJAMIN
Brodie. A Review of Sir B. Brodie's Letter on Homœopathy in 'Fraser's
Magazine,' with a Critical Investigation of the System. Demy 8vo,
sewed, 3d.

MASSY (Dr. R. TUTHILL) MILD MEDICINE IN CONTRADIS-
TINCTION to Severe Medicine. Second Edition. Cloth, 2s. 6d.

MONTHLY HOMŒOPATHIC REVIEW. Edited by Dr. RYAN. Posted
free to subscribers, as issued. Terms 12s. per annum. Single copies 1s.

    *** On and after 1st of January, 1862, each number will consist of sixty-
four pages instead of forty-eight as heretofore. This arrangement will enable
the editor to devote more space, not only to the usual original papers on the
literature and practice of Homœopathy, but also to notices of its passing
history, translations from foreign journals, and medical news generally.

    ☞ This serial is registered for transmission abroad, and therefore entitled
to all the privileges granted to newspapers, including the newspaper rate
of postage to all parts of the globe.

MOORE (Dr. G. L.) POPULAR GUIDE TO HOMŒOPATHY FOR
Families and Private Use. Second Edition. (Ten Thousand.) Limp
cloth, 1s.

    " A waistcoat-pocket encyclopædia on the subject."—*Manchester Weekly
Advertiser.*

MOORE (Dr. G. L.) SUPPLEMENT TO THE 'DOMESTIC PRACTICE
of Homœopathy,' being a companion to the various works thereon ;
containing information on a variety of subjects connected with, and bearing
on, the Family Practice of Homœopathy, but *not* treated of in the
Domestic Works on that subject—such as the Domestic Management of the
Sick-room, Conduct of Nurses and Attendants, Ventilation, Baths, Bandages,
Poultices, and Cookery for the Sick and Convalescent, &c., &c. Cloth,
2s. 6d.

    " No sick room should be without this useful little work, giving as it does
in a condensed form many most useful hints, which, if acted upon, will add
considerably to the comfort of the patient, and so hasten the recovery"

MOORE (Mr. JAS., V.S.) OUTLINES OF VETERINARY HOMŒO-
pathy. Comprising *Horse, Cow, Dog, Sheep,* and *Hog* Diseases, and their
Homœopathic Treatment. Second Edition, revised and enlarged by the
Author, with Additions. Cloth, 5s.

    " Eminently plain, practical, and useful."—*Liverpool Mercury.*
    " A concise and popular treatise, almost wholly divested of technical terms ;
such a book as no one with ordinary capacity can misunderstand."—*Irish
Farmer's Gazette.*
    " To farmers, both professional and amateur, the book will prove exceed-
ingly useful."—*Manchester Weekly Advertiser.*
    "Its directions for the selection of the remedy are precise and clear."—
Manchester Examiner and Times.
    " Mr. Moore's 'Outlines' are prepared with great judgment and care, and, in
the hands of a farmer of ordinary intelligence, the work will be a treasure."—
Monthly Homœopathic Review.

MOORE (Mr. JAS., V.S.) COMMON DISEASES OF ANIMALS,
and their Homœopathic Treatment ; carefully abridged from the ' Outlines
of Veterinary Homœopathy,' by the same Author. Cloth, 2s. 6d.

MOORE (Mr. JAS., V.S.) LUNG DISEASE OF CATTLE, OR PLEURO-
pneumonia Curable by Homœopathy, with directions for its Treatment.
Sixth Edition. Sewed, 6d.

MOORE (MR. JAS., V.S.) MILK FEVER OF COWS; ITS HOMŒO-
pathic Treatment and Cure, with directions. Second Edition. Sewed,
6d.

MOORE (MR. JAS., V.S.) VETERINARY HOMŒOPATHY, ILLUS-
trated by 125 Cases, selected from many years' practice in the Homœopathic
Treatment of Animals, with observations. Sewed, 6d.

   *** To those unacquainted with the method of treating animals Homœopathically, this pamphlet is of the greatest assistance.

MORGAN (DR. WILLIAM). DIPHTHERIA, ITS PATHOLOGY AND
Homœopathic Treatment, with Cases illustrative of its Cure. Sewed, 6d.

NOTES ON DOMESTIC HOMŒOPATHY. Sewed, 6d.

METCALF (DR. J. W.) HOMŒOPATHIC PROVINGS. An appendix to
the North American Journal of Homœopathy. Cloth, 7s. 6d.

METCALF (DR. J. W.) HOMŒOPATHY, AND ITS REQUIREMENTS
of the Physician. Sewed, 6d.

MORGAN (DR. SAMUEL,) TEXT BOOK FOR DOMESTIC PRACTICE.
Cloth, 1s.

NEIDHARD (DR. C.) CROTALUS HORRIDUS IN YELLOW FEVER,
also in Malignant, Bilious, and Remittent Fevers. With an account of
Humbolt's Prophylactic Inoculation of the Venom of a Serpent at Havanna,
Cuba. Cloth, 4s.

NORTH AMERICAN JOURNAL OF HOMŒOPATHY. A Quarterly
Magazine of Medicine and the Auxillary Sciences. Price 3s. 6d. Posted
free to Subscribers on the arrival of the first mail after its publication in
New York for 14s. per an., payable in advance.

NORTON (DR. J. E.) HOMŒOPATHIC FAMILY MEDICINE. Second
Edition, revised and enlarged. Cloth, 2s. 6d.

PATHOGENETIC CYCLOPÆDIA PART I, CONTAINING SYMP-
toms of the Head, Mind, and Disposition. By Dr. Dudgeon. Cloth,
18s., or to Subscribers to the New Repertory, 10s. 6d.

PEARCE (DR. A. C.) DIARRHŒA AND CHOLERA. Their Homœopathic
Treatment and Prevention briefly described. Sewed, 6d.

PEARCE (Dr. A. C.) THE MEDICAL PRACTITIONER'S BILL OF
1858. A brief analysis of its Oppressive and Unconstitutional clauses.
Sewed, 3d.

PETERS (DR. J. C.) A TREATISE ON HEADACHES: INCLUDING
Acute, Chronic, Nervous, Gastric, Dyspeptic, or Sick Headaches ; also,
Congestive, Rheumatic, and Periodical Headaches. Based on Th. J.
Rückert's "Clinical experience in Homœopathy." Cloth, 4s.

PETERS (DR. J. C.) A TREATISE ON APOPLEXY. With an Appendix
on Softening of the Brain and Paralysis. Based on Th. J. Rückert's
"Clinical Experience in Homœopathy." Cloth, 4s.

PETERS (DR. J. C.) A TREATISE ON THE DISEASES OF MARRIED
Females. Disorders of Pregnancy, Parturition and Lactation. Cloth, 4s.

PETERS (Dr. J. C.) A TREATISE ON DISEASES OF THE EYES.
Based on Th. J. Rückert's "Clinical Experience in Homœopathy.
Cloth, 4s.

PETERS (Dr. J. C.) A TREATISE ON INTERNAL DISEASES OF THE
Eyes; including Diseases of the Iris, Crystalline Lens, Choroid Retina,
and Optic Nerve. Based on Th. J. Rückert's "Clinical Experience in
Homœopathy." Cloth, 4s.

PETERS (Dr. J. C.) A TREATISE ON THE INFLAMMATORY AND
Organic Diseases of the Brain. Based on Th. J. Rückert's "Clinical
Experience in Homœopathy." Cloth, 4s.

PETERS (Dr. J. C.) A TREATISE ON NERVOUS DERANGEMENTS
and Mental Disorders. Based on Th. J. Rückert's "Clinical Experience
in Homœopathy." Cloth, 4s.

PETERS (Dr. J. C.) A COMPLETE TREATISE ON HEADACHES AND
Diseases of the Head. 1. The Nature and Treatment of Headaches; 2.
The Nature and Treatment of Apoplexy; 3. The Nature and Treatment
of Mental Derangement; 4. The Nature and Treatment of Irritation,
Congestion, and Inflammation of the Brain and its Membranes. Based on
T. J. Rückert's "Clinical Experience in Homœopathy." Cloth, 4s.

PETERS (Dr. J. C.) THE SCIENCE AND ART, OR THE PRINCIPLES
and Practice of Medicine. Issued in Numbers, of 96 pages each; the
whole work may reach 21 Numbers. Price of each Number, 3s. Parts I
to VI have already been received.

POPE (Dr. A. C.) ETHICAL IMPEDIMENTS TO THE PROGRESS
of Homœopathy throughout the Profession. Sewed, 6d.

POPE (Dr. A. C.) THE HOMŒOPATHIC SYSTEM OF MEDICINE;
its Theory and Results examined and compared with those of other Methods
of Treatment. Sewed, 6d.

POPULAR HOMŒOPATHIC TRACTS. Sewed, 6d.

PRINCIPAL USES OF THE SIXTEEN MOST IMPORTANT HO-
mœopathic Medicines. Limp cloth, 2s.

PULTE (Dr. J. H.) WOMAN'S MEDICAL GUIDE; CONTAINING
Essays on the Physical, Moral and Educational Development of Females,
and the Homœopathic Treatment of their Diseases in all Periods of Life;
together with Directions for the Remedial Use of Water and Gymnastics.
Cloth, 7s.

RANSFORD (Dr. C.) PREVENTION AND TREATMENT OF SCAR-
latina in its various forms, according to Homœopathic Principles.
Sewed, 2d.

RAPOU (Dr. AUG.). TREATISE ON TYPHOID FEVER, AND ITS
Homœopathic Treatment. Translated from the French by Arthur Alleyn
Granville. Cloth, 3s.

RAU (Dr. G. L.) ORGANON OF THE SPECIFIC HEALING ART
of Homœopathy. Translated by C. J. Hempel, M.D. Cloth, 6s. 6d.

REASONS FOR ADOPTING HOMŒOPATHIC TREATMENT IN
the Diseases of Animals. Sewed, 2d.

REED (Dr. D. McCONNELL). REASONS FOR EMBRACING HO-
mœopathy, and Impediments to the more General Success of the Practice.
In stiff cover, 2s.

REIL (Dr.) MONOGRAPH UPON ACONITE—ITS USES, TO-
gether with Accurate Statements derived from various sources. A
Prize Essay Translated from the German by Dr H. B. MILLARD. Cloth,
3s. 6d.

REMARKS ON SIR BENJAMIN BRODIE'S LETTER ON HO-
mœopathy in 'Fraser's Magazine' for September, 1861. (Reprinted
from the 'British Journal of Homœopathy' for October, 1861.) Demy 8vo,
sewed, 6d.

REPERTORY (THE NEW); OR SYSTEMATIC ARRANGEMENT AND
Analysis of the Homœopathic Materia Medica. This work is expected to
be completed in about six or eight parts, five of which are already
published. Post free to subscribers for 4s. per part; to non-subscribers
the price per part is 5s.

ROKITANSKY'S PATHOLOGICAL ANATOMY. Translated from the
German, with Additions on Diagnosis, from Schöulein, Skoda, and others.
By Dr. J. C. PETERS. Cloth, 4s.

ROTH (Dr. M.) THE PREVENTION OF SPINAL DEFORMITIES,
especially of Lateral Curvatures. Illustrated. Cloth, 3s. 6d.

ROTH (Dr. M.) THE PREVENTION AND CURE OF MANY CHRONIC
Diseases by Movements. Illustrated. Cloth, 10s.

ROUFF'S REPERTORY OF HOMŒOPATHIC MEDICINE, NOSO-
logically arranged. Translated from the German by A. H. Okie, M.D.,
Translator of "Hartmann's Remedies." Second American Edition,
with Additions and Improvements, by Dr. G. Humphrey. Cloth, 7s. 6d.

RUSH'S HANDBOOK TO VETERINARY HOMŒOPATHY. Cloth,
2s. 6d.

SCHLÆFER'S VETERINARY HOMŒOPATHY. Translated from the
German, and edited, with additions, by C. J. HEMPEL, M.D. Cloth,
6s. 6d.

SHERILL'S MANUAL OF HOMŒOPATHIC PRESCRIPTION, with
an Improved Repertory; also an Introduction, in which the Doctrine and
Nature of the Homœopathic System is explained. 1s. 6d.

SHERILL (Dr. H.) A TREATISE ON HOMŒOPATHIC PRACTICE
of Medicine. Comprised in a Repertory for Prescribing, adapted to
Domestic Use. Third Edition, improved and enlarged. Cloth, 5s.

SMALL (Dr. A. E.) MANUAL OF HOMŒOPATHIC PRACTICE.
Seventh enlarged Edition. Cloth, 10s.

SMALL (Dr. A. E.) THE POCKET MANUAL OF HOMŒOPATHIC
Practice. Abridged from the 'Manual of Homœopathic Practice,' by
Dr. J. F. Sheek. Cloth, 2s.

SMITH (Rev. F.) HOMŒOPATHY, AND ITS ADVANTAGES TO
the Working Classes; a Lecture delivered in Turner Street Schools,
Manchester. Sewed 3d.

SMITH (Dr. J. H.) FACTS IN EVIDENCE OF THE TRUTH OF
Homœopathy. Being an account of *fifty cases successfully treated* on
that principle, with remarks. Sewed, 6d.

SNELLING (Dr. F. G.) THE HOMŒOPATHIC TREATMENT OF
Diptheria. Sewed, 1s.

STAPF (Dr. E.) ADDITION TO THE MATERIA MEDICA PURA.
Translated by Dr. C. J. Hempel. Cloth, 7s. 6d.

TARBELL (Dr. J. À.) SOURCES OF HEALTH, AND THE PRE-
vention of Disease. Cloth, 2s. 6d.

TEN REASONS WHY I PREFER HOMŒOPATHY TO THE COMMON
System of Medical Treatment. By the Father of a Family. Third
Edition. (Thirty Thousand.) In wrapper, 2d.

TESSIER (Dr. J. P.) CLINICAL RESEARCHES CONCERNING THE
Homœopathic Treatment of Asiatic Cholera. Translated by Dr. C. J.
Hempel. Cloth, 4s.

TESTE (Dr. A.) THE HOMŒOPATHIC MATERIA MEDICA, arranged
Systematically and Practically. Translated by Dr. J. C. Hempel. Cloth,
12s. 6d.

TESTE (Dr. A.) A HOMŒOPATHIC TREATISE ON THE DISEASES
of Children. Translated by Emma H. Côte. Cloth, 5s. 6d.

THOMAS (Dr. H.) ADDITIONS TO THE HOMŒOPATHIC MA-
teria Medica; with explanations and remarks respecting the Provings of
Homœopathic Medicines. Limp cloth, 2s. 6d.

THOMAS (Dr. H.) DISEASES OF CHILDREN, AND THEIR HO-
mœopathic Treatment. Compiled from the works of Teste, Hartmann,
Williamson, and others, with additions. Cloth, 3s.

THOMAS (Dr. H.) EXTERNAL REMEDIES IN CASES OF ACCIDENT,
&c. Third Edition, illustrated. Limp cloth, 1s.

TURNER (Mr. HENRY) ON THE FOOD OF YOUNG INFANTS;
or, Wet Nurses and Hand-feeding Superseded by the Discovery of a
true and exact Analogue of the Human Milk. Reprinted from No. LXI
of the 'British Journal of Homœopathy.' Sewed, 2d.

TURNER'S ILLUSTRATED AND DESCRIPTIVE GUIDE IN THE
selection of a Homœopathic Medicine Chest. Post free on application.

UNITED STATES JOURNAL OF HOMŒOPATHY. Quarterly, 4s. Post-free to Subscribers on the arrival of each number for 16s. per annum, payable in advance.

WATTERS' HOMŒOPATHIC CHART. Giving the Symptoms and Remedies for Diseases coming more particularly under Domestic Treatment. In cloth case, 1s. 6d.; in sheet, 1s.

WILLIAMSON (DR. WALTER). DISEASES OF FEMALES AND their Homœopathic Treatment; containing also a full description of the Dose of each Medicine. Second English Edition. Cloth, 2s.

WOLF (DR. C. W.) APIS-MELLIFICA; OR, THE POISON OF THE Honey-Bee, considered as a Therapeutic Agent. In stiff cover, 1s. 6d.

YELDHAM (S., M.R.C.S.) THE MORAL EVIDENCES OF HOMŒO-pathy. Two Lectures delivered at the Homœopathic Hospital. Sewed, 6d.

YELDHAM (S., M.R.C.S.) REMARKS ON THE DIFFERENT MODES of administering Homœopathic Medicines, with a view to the disuse of the Globule. Sewed, 3d.

YELDHAM (S., M.R.C.S.) ARNICA, RHUS, AND CALENDULA. A Lecture on 'Surgery as Modified by Homœopathy,' delivered at the London Homœopathic Hospital. Sewed, 6d.

YOUNG (DR. G. H.) HOMŒOPATHY, WHAT IT IS, AND WHY IT should be adopted. Sewed, 6d.

New Books and Pamphlets on Homœopathy published in this country are supplied as soon as issued, and New American Works, imported as soon as possible after their issue, are punctually supplied on their arrival.

HENRY TURNER AND CO.,

Homœopathic Chemists and Medical Publishers,

77, FLEET STREET, LONDON, E.C.,

AND

41, PICCADILLY, AND 15, MARKET STREET, MANCHESTER.

www.ingramcontent.com/pod-product-compliance
Lightning Source LLC
Chambersburg PA
CBHW031114020726
47495CB00007B/2200